BROKEN PROMISE

Simon Toyne is the bestselling author of the *Sanctus* trilogy: *Sanctus*, *The Key* and *The Tower*. He wrote *Sanctus* after quitting his job as a TV executive to focus on writing. It was the biggest-selling debut thriller of 2011 in the UK and an international bestseller. His books have been translated into 27 languages and published in over 50 countries.

Simon lives with his family in Brighton and the South of France.

simontoyne.net
 Facebook.com/simon.toyne.writer
 Follow him on Twitter @simontoyne

Also by Simon Toyne

The Boy Who Saw
Solomon Creed
Sanctus
The Key
The Tower

BROKEN PROMISE

SIMON TOYNE

FEATURING SOLOMON CREED

HarperCollins*Publishers*

HarperCollins*Publishers*
1 London Bridge Street
London SE1 9GF

www.harpercollins.co.uk

This paperback edition 2018

First published in Great Britain in ebook format by
HarperCollins*Publishers* 2018

A catalogue record for this book
is available from the British Library

ISBN: 978-0-00-830866-7

Set in Minion by Palimpsest Book Production Limited,
Falkirk, Stirlingshire

Printed and bound by CPI Group (UK) Ltd, Croydon, CR0 4YY

MIX
Paper from
responsible sources
FSC
www.fsc.org   FSC™ C007454

This is for my readers.
Without you I'm just a crazy person
sitting alone in a room.

1

Solomon Creed walked east, away from Arizona and all the complications that spilt blood tends to bring. He kept to the minor roads and travelled mostly at night, dodging the traffic and the sledgehammer sun, sipping water from a plastic gallon jug he'd found crumpled in a roadside ditch outside Bisbee.

He tipped it up now and drank the blood-warm water until the jug was empty. He could fill it again at the next gas station, or diner, or truck stop. Water was not a problem. You could pick up water for free if you stuck to the roads. But not food. Food you had to pay for, or take what you could find, baked and rancid by the side of the road.

On day one it had been a cottontail that had been clipped by a car then limped off to die in the shade of an ephedra bush. He'd skinned and gutted it using the jagged edge of a broken beer bottle then roasted it over a small fire coaxed from mesquite straw using the same bottle and the sun's fierce rays. Day two was a rattlesnake he'd disturbed in a storm drain while taking shelter from the rising heat. It had struck from the shadows, the rattle coming at the same time as the fangs. Solomon had felt

1

the minute shift in air pressure and twitched out of the way, catching it behind the head, grabbing its tail then cracking it like a bullwhip, so sharp that it snapped the head clean off. He had drunk its blood, the bitter warmth soaking life back into his tired muscles, then gutted it and chewed slowly on its cooling flesh. He had a fleeting memory of doing something similar in a different desert, but like most memories regarding himself, it was gone before he could catch a hold of it. He had sat cross-legged, in the dusty dark, licking snake blood from his fingers and sucking the warm, viscous contents of the leathery eggs the mother had been laying. That had been thirty-six hours ago now. The only things that had passed his lips since were air and water so hot from the jug you could brew tea with it. But there was something up ahead, something carried on the wind and getting stronger with each step he took. It was the smell of hot grease and salt, fried potatoes and ham, eggs and coffee, and his stomach rumbled in response whenever the wind shifted. He had smelled similar at every greasy-windowed truck stop he'd passed along the way and had always got no further than the parking lot, the need to catch another ride and put distance between himself and Arizona stronger than his hunger. But Arizona was four days, hundreds of miles and a state and a half behind him now. And his legs ached and his stomach growled and the thought of another road-kill meal washed down with plastic-tasting water made him feel sick to his empty stomach. The problem was no longer urgency, it was economic. Because a sit-down meal with seasoning and sauces, and iced-water on the side, would cost money and the only coin he had to his name was a single, worn-down quarter he'd found by a city limits sign a hundred miles or more back.

He reached into the pocket of the pale suit jacket he wore and palmed the quarter, rolling it over his knuckles as smoothly as he rolled the problem of his poverty over and over in his mind until he saw a skinny tower rise up ahead on the eastbound side of the I-10. Red neon letters burned on the side spelling out '*BOBBY D's EATS*', and an arrow buzzed below it, pointing down to a one-storey building surrounded by dusty cars and big rigs.

Solomon left the highway and walked through lines of trucks with confederate flags and the silhouettes of pneumatic women on their mud-flaps. He passed a boarded-up gas station with decommissioned pumps and a printed sheet of paper taped to the door announcing that the place was due to be sold at auction on July 21st along with some land. He had no idea what day it was but the diner was still open and cooking food, which was all that mattered to him right now. He dropped the empty gallon jug by the door and stepped inside.

A bell tinkled above his head and a couple of sets of eyes peered up beneath the brims of battered caps before returning to their plates of food, finding their steaks and ribs more interesting than the tall, dusty dude who had just blown in. There were maybe fifteen guys spread out in a place that could easily seat eighty. Not exactly busy but busy enough for what Solomon had in mind.

He took in the room, his senses overwhelmed after so long spent outside on wide, empty roads. Booths lined three of the walls and a long counter stretched along the fourth, ending at a dusty display cabinet displaying Indian beads, souvenir caps and T-shirts with the slogan '*A gift from Broken Promise, Texas*' stitched across them. A sun-faded photograph hung above it showing Native American symbols – eagles and moons, stick horses and arrows – carved into the rough ochre walls of what looked like a cave. People were reading newspapers or chatting in groups. No one was looking at their phones. A sign by the cash register explained why. '*We don't got free Internet so don't ask*', it said. *Perfect*, Solomon thought, and headed over to the counter, feeling the greasy air and the tickle of stolen glances on his skin.

Low conversations murmured and blurred with the tinny whine of a country and western song. The clatter and sizzle of the kitchen and the smell of grease and the salt-sour odour of unwashed bodies hung thick in the air. He pulled out a stool from the middle of the counter and savoured the exquisite relief of sitting after so long on his feet. He stretched his legs and arched his back. The menu was painted on the wall behind the counter, the blue paint of the lettering faded and cracked by age and heat. There were dollar bills pinned to the wall too, marked with messages from the people who'd left them – '*Big Bear blew thru*', '*This buck stops here*', '*Bobby D's – best breakfast in West Texas*'. A plastic tumbler clacked down on the beaten metal counter and iced water rattled into it like rocks into a bucket.

'If it's on the wall, we got it. If it ain't we don't, so don't bother asking.' The waitress was tall and whip-thin, black-blue hair pulled into a ponytail and skin like caramel against the ice-cream pink of her uniform. Her name badge said '*Hi I'm Rita*'.

'Is Bobby D around?' Solomon asked.

'Bobby D's dead,' the woman said flatly.

'Then who's the owner?'

She fixed him with her green eyes. 'If you got a complaint or you're fixing to sell something I ain't interested. And if you're looking to buy you're a day early. Auction's tomorrow morning.'

She had Irish eyes, though her honeyed skin showed her people had been here far longer than any European. 'You're the owner,' Solomon said.

She shrugged. 'Until tomorrow I am.'

'Then why didn't you ever change the sign?'

The water jug came to rest on the counter and Solomon thought about the river of iced-water that must have flowed from it over the years, a river that would end tomorrow with the fall of an auctioneer's hammer.

4

'Don't need my name on the place to know I own it,' she said. 'And new neon costs money I ain't got. You going to order something or not? There's a cover charge either way.'

'Actually I have a proposition,' Solomon said, loud enough to draw the room's attention. 'A wager.'

Rita stared at him like he'd just cursed. 'Gambling's illegal in the state of Texas.'

Solomon nodded. 'In general, yes, but not if it's classed as social gambling.'

The green eyes narrowed. 'And what would that be?'

'It's a bet undertaken in a private place such as this, with an element of skill involved, not just chance, where the only person to receive any benefit is the winner of the wager, meaning the house takes no cut.'

Rita nodded. 'Sounds fancy. You a lawyer?'

Solomon shook his head. 'I don't think so.'

'You don't *think* so? You don't know if you're a lawyer but you're giving me chapter and verse on the law regarding gambling in the state of Texas?' She shook her head. 'Sounds off to me. I ain't interested, mister. You let me know when you're ready to order.' She turned and walked away, banging the water jug down hard on the end of the counter before disappearing through the old-style saloon doors into the kitchen.

Solomon's stomach growled again in response to the smell of food hanging in the air and he took a long drink to try and silence it, the coldness flooding through him and the ice chips bumping against his lips. It would have been better for him if Bobby D had still been around. Men were easier to hook where wagers were concerned, their egos making it hard for them to back down from another man's challenge. Maybe he'd have to take his chances out on the road again, find another diner that wasn't owned by an Indian warrior princess with Irish eyes.

He drained his glass, placed it down on the counter ready to leave and felt the air shift and thicken to his left as someone moved closer. Then a low voice laced with nicotine and coffee murmured, 'What kind of a wager?'

2

Solomon turned and took in the tattooed trucker perched on the edge of the neighbouring stool. He was leaning in and peering up from beneath the brim of his cap, his body language telegraphing his eagerness to swallow the bait Solomon had laid.

'Wager is that I can answer any three questions you care to ask me.'

The trucker nodded as if Solomon's answer confirmed what he already knew. 'Any three questions at all?'

'Anything.'

The trucker continued to nod. 'What's the stake?'

'If I answer correctly you buy me dinner.'

'That it?'

'That's it.'

'And what do I get if you don't?'

Solomon slapped his hand down on the counter. 'This.' He took it away to reveal the worn quarter beneath.

The trucker stared at the silver coin and frowned. 'Twenty-five cents!?'

'Not exactly. Look at the date.'

The trucker leaned in and peered at the numbers stamped beneath George Washington's profile. 'Nineteen seventy-six. So what?'

'So that's a bicentennial quarter,' Solomon kept his voice low as if he was sharing valuable information, 'minted to commemorate two hundred years of American independence. Much higher silver to nickel ratio than a regular quarter. Feel the weight of it.'

The trucker picked up the coin with fat, oil-cracked fingers then cupped it in the callused ham of his hand. 'Feels like a regular quarter to me.'

'Well it's not. It's slightly heavier – and a lot more valuable.'

The silver coin shone dully in the rough hand. 'What's it worth?'

'A rare coin dealer will give you two hundred dollars for one in mint condition.'

The trucker let out a low whistle then frowned. 'Yeah but this ain't mint. This coin just about worn away to nuthin.'

Solomon nodded. 'Which is why you'll only get a hundred dollars for it.'

'A hunnert bucks for this?'

'Maybe more. Certainly not less.'

'And you're willing to stake it against a fifteen-dollar meal?' Solomon nodded. The trucker stared at the coin then shook his head and put it down on the counter. 'I don't know. There's a catch. I cain't see what it is but I know there is one. Has to be.'

'I'll take that bet.' A skinny man in a rancher's shirt stepped in front of the trucker and thrust out his hand at Solomon. 'Name's Billy-Joe. Billy-Joe Redford.'

Solomon took the hand and shook it. It was work-hardened and strong, hard lines from lanyards worn into the skin. 'Pleased to meet you, Billy-Joe.'

'Now hold on,' the trucker said, standing up from his stool. 'I never said I weren't taking the bet.'

'Sure sounded that way to me,' Billy-Joe peered down at the coin on the counter. 'What d'ya say this was?'

'Bicentennial,' Solomon replied. 'Very collectible.'

'And worth a hunnert bucks to a collector, you say?'

Solomon nodded. 'Maybe more.'

Billy-Joe smiled. 'Sure, I'll buy it. You got yourself a deal, mister. I'll stand you a steak if you can answer three questions.'

'Now wait a second,' the trucker dumped his hand on the cowboy's shoulder and spun him round. 'You can't just muscle in on another man's deal like that. Man was talking to me first.'

'And now he's talkin' to me.' The cowboy stepped closer to the trucker and looked up. The trucker was six inches taller and double the weight, though neither fact seemed to faze the cowboy. The silence stretched between them.

A loud bang broke the tension and everybody turned to the source. Rita was standing at the end of the counter, a water jug in her hand slopping ice over the side from the force of being banged on the counter. 'Far as I recall the gentleman was talking to me first.'

'Yeah, Rita, but you done passed on the wager,' Billy-Joe said, still staring up at the trucker. 'Same way this joker did. Only one that's shaken the man's hand on it is me.' He glanced at Solomon. 'Ain't that right, mister . . .?'

'Creed,' Solomon said. 'Solomon Creed. And you're right. You are the only one who has accepted my wager. However,' he looked at Rita. 'I do not wish to be the cause of any trouble here. It's your house, your rules. If you want me to move on and drop the whole thing then that's what I'll do.'

There was a groan from the crowd and Rita looked around at the assembled group, their expectations hanging in the greasy air like something solid. She looked about ready to kick everyone out but then a new voice piped up from the back of the room.

'Let these fellas settle it.'

The crowd shifted and turned to look at the new speaker. He was sitting in a booth on the back wall, reading a newspaper like an old timer, though he couldn't have been more than thirty. He was compact and solid-looking in a way that suggested hours in the gym rather than hard days working the land. He wore a dark blue, check work shirt that had been tailored to fit and his mouse-brown hair was well cut and slicked back to keep it out of his face.

'He's right about the law,' the man said, slowly folding his paper and laying it flat on the table, like he was accustomed to being both listened to and making people wait. 'Ain't no crime if folks want to have a wager in a privately owned house, providing that house don't benefit in any way financial.' He looked over at Rita. 'I say let these boys have their wager. Make a change from hearing the same damned twelve songs on the juke at least.'

Rita stood for a moment, her hand clenched tight around the handle of the water jug like she was maybe thinking about throwing it at him. Then she relaxed and let go of the jug. 'Do what you want,' she said, heading back into the kitchen. 'This time tomorrow none of this will be my problem anyway.'

A murmur of approval rippled through the circle of onlookers as almost everybody in the place now abandoned their meals and clustered round the counter.

'All right then,' Billy-Joe said, pulling up a stool and rubbing his hands together like a kid about to tuck into a piece of chocolate cake. 'Looks like we got ourselves a game.' He waited for the crowd to settle then took a deep breath and fixed Solomon with his best poker stare.

'OK, Mister Creed,' he said. 'Here comes my first question.'

3

'So my mom's favourite singer of all time was Julie London. Man, she loved that gal – way more than any of the dudes she ever brung home. Anyways whenever those dudes up and left again she'd always get drunk and play *Love on the Rocks* over and over – not the song, you understand, I mean the whole damn album. Consequently I know that damn album way better'n any red-blooded man oughta. So my question to you is,' Billy-Joe paused for effect and a smile crept across his face. 'What is the name of the fifth track on side two?'

Another murmur passed through the crowd and heads were shaken. If anybody had any idea what the answer might be they certainly weren't going to own up to it.

Solomon ran a finger down the side of his empty water glass and sucked the condensation off it, focusing on the torrent of information rushing through his mind in response to the question, a river of facts about Julie London, her life, career and recording history. He had discovered, in the few days he could actually remember, that information came so easily to him that it was as much of an effort to filter out the things that were not relevant as it was to decide what was. But there was also a bitter twist to this almost bottomless gift of knowledge. Because the one thing he truly desired to know above all else was about himself, and on that subject he knew almost nothing. The only reason he knew his name was because it was stitched into the label of the tailor-made jacket he wore. But if he looked in a mirror he did not recognize the man staring back at him, though ask the stranger in the mirror anything else, anything at all, and he knew the answer instantly: even the identity of an obscure statue in an even more obscure town.

'"The Man That Got Away"', Solomon said. 'The fifth track on side two of *Love on the Rocks* by Julie London is "The Man That Got Away".'

There was a silence punctuated only by murmured questions and the low, steady drone of the jukebox.

Billy-Joe stared at Solomon for a long second before his poker face cracked and a smile exploded across it. 'Damn,' he said. 'How in the hell do you know a thing like that?'

'Is he right?' people asked in the crowd. 'Did he get it right?'

'Hell yeah he got it right,' Billy-Joe said, and the room exploded into noise.

'Looks like you need to up your game, son,' someone shouted, then he turned to the crowd. 'And if anyone wants a little side action, I got twenty bucks says this fella's going to answer whatever questions Billy-Joe throws at him.'

'I'll take that bet,' someone replied, and the room hummed louder as more bets were placed.

Billy-Joe sat quiet and still on his stool, staring at Solomon like he was a puzzle to be solved. Solomon just stared ahead, scanning the menu on the wall and doing his best to ignore the hunger gnawing at his stomach.

When the room settled Billy-Joe rubbed his hands together

12

like before. 'OK,' he said. 'I figure any man can answer an obscure question about Julie London ain't likely to be too interested in sports, so let me pitch this one atcha.' He paused, waiting for complete silence in the diner before speaking again. 'In nineteen and seventy-eight,' he said, keeping his voice low, 'there was a ballgame 'tween the Rangers and the Baltimore Orioles. Now during that game an Orioles fan had a heart attack and was gonna die right there in the stands, only one of the players jumped up off of the bench and saved that man's life. What I want to know – is the name of that ball player.'

A murmur rippled through the crowd and heads shook. Solomon stared at the menu on the wall and focused on the information pouring through his head in response to the cowboy's question:

Texas Rangers . . . 1978 season . . . finished second in the ALW behind the Kansas City Royals . . .

The information began to take shape now, forming vague images like half-forgotten memories as his mind sank deeper into the details.

. . . evening of July 17th . . . away game at the Baltimore Memorial Stadium . . . grey skies but still summer warm and close, like a storm was coming . . . the game is halted in the seventh when a shout goes up behind the Orioles dugout . . .

Solomon's mind continued to freefall through clouds of facts until they formed images, as if he was remembering something he had once witnessed himself:

. . . the crowd behind the dugout form a circle, their attention on the centre and not on the field. The shout goes out again, clearer this time: 'A doctor. This man needs a doctor.' The man who shouts looks around, eyes white and frantic. Another man lies at his feet. Big guy. Not moving. Nobody comes forward. Time slides to a halt . . .

*. . . 1978 . . . July . . . Jimmy Carter in the White House . . .
Grease playing to packed houses in the movie theatres . . . 1978,
when ballplayers still earned regular pay cheques and had second
careers.*

*The silence is broken. 'Here,' someone calls out and there's
movement in the away team dugout as one of the Rangers' pitchers
stands, moves to the edge of the field and vaults over the guardrail.
The crowd parts as he climbs the seats and watches on as he drops
down by the big guy. This pitcher has one good season left and
knows it. He's in his second year residency at a Pittsburgh hospital.
He administers CPR to the stricken fan like he's done a hundred
times in the ER and mouth-to-mouth like he was taught. The fan
coughs and groans and the pitcher keeps working steadily, pumping
his chest, hand-over-hand, working the heart now he's breathing
again, keeping it going until the ambulance arrives. The fan's
name was Germain. Germain Languth. And the Rangers' pitcher
was called:*

'Medich,' Solomon said and turned to the cowboy. 'George
"Doc" Medich. He saved the man's life and the game was resumed.
The Rangers went on to win two to nothing.'

There was a pause as the whole room held its breath. Billy-Joe
stared at Solomon in disbelief. 'Now how in the hell did you
know that?'

The room erupted into noise and money was waved in the air
as more side bets went down. Some still bet against Solomon,
but the majority were now with him. Hands were shaken and
attention turned back to the dusty stranger at the centre of it all.

There was one question left and the cowboy looked edgy, his
eyes darting around the room as he tried to come up with a
question that might still win him the bet. Solomon stared ahead
at the menu. Steak and eggs and home fries, that's what he would
order. Or maybe the special, whatever that was. His stomach

growled in anticipation, lost in the hubbub of the room. One more question.

Then the trucker stood up with a sharp scrape of metal on concrete and pointed his thick finger at Solomon. 'I see the angle now,' he swung the finger round to Billy-Joe and poked him in the chest. 'You're working together, ain't ya? You two's grifters. This whole goddam thing's a set-up.'

4

Billy-Joe spun away from the trucker's finger and squared up to him. 'What you just call me?'

The trucker jabbed the finger into his chest again. 'I said this here's a con and you two's workin' it together. How in the hell else could he answer a question like that?'

Billy-Joe looked up with the same cold challenge as previously. 'So how's this con work then, genius? You think we travel around Texas hitting diners so that I can deliberately lose a bet to someone I'm secretly workin' with? Where's the grift in that?'

The trucker pointed at the crowd. 'I bet you got a third guy, ain't ya, whippin' up interest and layin' down some side bets?'

'Bullshit,' Billy-Joe said and bumped his chest against the trucker's.

The trucker pulled himself up to his full height and glared down at the cowboy, holding his ground, the eyes of the crowd upon them. No one saw Rita step out of the kitchen and pop the cash register, though they all heard the crash it made when she slammed it shut again. The hollow clang echoed away in the silence that followed and Rita moved away from the register, looking around the room and making sure everyone felt the full weight of her disapproval.

'I didn't ask for you boys to start waving your dicks around over some stupid ass bet.' She shot a glance to the back of the room where the man in the booth was back to reading his newspaper. 'But if y'all are gonna start pickin' fights then I'm puttin' a stop to this thing right now.'

A collective groan went up in the room and a short, round man in a Coors Light T-shirt stepped forward. 'Aw come on now Rita, that ain't fair.' He held his sweat-stained rancher's hat in front of him like he was pleading for his soul on a Sunday. 'Just 'cause these two's gettin' all worked up, don't mean the rest of us have to suffer none. I say let the cowboy ask his last question.'

A murmur of agreement rippled through the crowd.

'I still say it's a con,' the trucker muttered.

'Then don't put any damn money down,' the man in the Coors Light T-shirt said. 'But don't be ruining things for the rest of us.'

The trucker puffed himself up again and turned to face this new challenger as the noise in the room started to rise.

'If I may,' a voice cut through the noise, so calm it was as distinct as a shout. All eyes turned to Solomon. 'Might I suggest a solution.' He turned to the room. 'You all want to see if I can answer the last question.' There was a general nodding and murmurs of agreement. Solomon turned to the trucker. 'But you don't trust Billy-Joe here to ask it?'

The trucker shook his head. 'No,' he said, 'I do not.'

Solomon looked over at Rita now. 'And you just want this to be over.'

Rita said nothing, but it was clear which direction her opinion lay.

'Then why don't you ask the last question? Everyone knows you here, I assume, so no one will think you're working with me

17

on some kind of con. So you ask the question, I'll try and answer it, the wager will end, one way or another, and everyone will get what they want.'

The mutterings started up again and Billy-Joe frowned as he took in the proposal. 'But if you ask the last question and he cain't answer it, who gets the quarter?'

'You can have it,' Rita said. 'And if he gets it right I'll stand him a meal on the house. That work for ya?'

Billy-Joe nodded slowly. 'Yeah, sure. I guess.' He looked up at the trucker. 'You OK with that?' The trucker frowned hard as he tried to figure out the new angle and when he couldn't see one he nodded and sat back down on his stool.

'And no more damn bets,' Rita said, lifting the hatch in the counter and stepping out into the main diner area. 'Let's get this thing over with so we can all get back to our dull, uneventful days. Can't handle all this excitement on a Wednesday lunchtime.' She strode across the floor to the display case of Native American souvenirs, snatched the framed photograph from the wall above it then walked back to the counter. 'Here's my question,' she said, and laid the photograph down on the counter in front of Solomon. 'Tell me what that says.'

The room went quiet as Solomon looked down at the photograph. It had been taken in a cave, the flash of the camera lighting the centre but falling away to a deep black at the edges. Some of the symbols had caught shadow, showing that they were petroglyphs, carved into the rock not painted on the surface, meaning the message they carried was important. Solomon studied the symbols and opened his mind ready for the usual flood of facts that came in answer to any question. But this time was different. This time the information that came was indistinct and inconclusive, more like a bank of fog than a clear flowing river, and in the silence of the room he caught a whisper, one man confiding to another at the edge of the crowd. 'He ain't gonna answer it,' the voice said. 'That's written in Suma and ain't a man alive as can read it.'

Solomon focused on the symbols, using the word he'd overheard to shine new light on them:

Suma . . . Zuma . . . nomadic hunter-gatherers . . . descended from the Mogollon peoples . . . first mentioned in 1630 in despatches regarding Franciscan missions . . . allied themselves with the Spanish and gave land for Catholic missions in exchange for help in subduing their main rivals the Apache . . . the Spanish converted some of the Zuma and betrayed the rest . . . last known Zuma brave died in 1869 and the native language was lost . . . scholars believe it may have been Uto-Aztecan or maybe Athabaskan . . .

Solomon tried translating the symbols using each of these languages in turn. Neither made sense. He needed more information.

'Where was this photo taken?' he asked.

'About a mile north of here,' Rita replied, her green eyes studying Solomon with curiosity. 'There's a system of old caves on the edge of this land. Why you askin'?'

'Because different peoples have different meanings for things depending on where they come from.' Solomon held up the photograph and pointed to a symbol near the bottom of the message. 'This one, for example, the broken arrow. To the Northern Suma it means peace, but to the Western Suma it means a broken promise. Now I'm guessing it *is* Western Suma, and that's how this place got its name, but I wanted to check before I answered the question. There is a steak dinner riding on it after all.'

The hum in the room deepened and smiles spread on the faces of those who'd bet on the stranger.

Solomon's eyes drifted across the markings, their meanings emerging clearly now he could filter it through the knowledge of their origin.

'It's an agreement,' he said, 'between a man named Three Arrows in the Wind and a white man from across the great sea to the east – European, I'm guessing. It doesn't say the man's name but he's represented here by a symbol that looks like the head of a cow or maybe a buffalo.' Rita stiffened and Solomon looked up. 'You know who that is?'

She nodded. 'The conquistador who first came here in 1534 was a man named Álvar Núñez Cabeza deVaca. Cabeza deVaca is Spanish for . . .'

'Cow's head,' Solomon said, finishing her thought. He looked back at the photograph, translating the symbols easily now as his eyes drifted over the petroglyphs. 'DeVaca did a deal with the chief in this area. He was promised safe passage across these lands, everything from the Snake River in the south, to Two Bears Pass in the west, Three Arrows Cave to the north, and Flat Rock to the east.' Solomon looked up at Rita. 'Do those landmarks mean anything to you?'

She nodded. 'They used to call the Rio Grande Snake River on account of the way it meanders through the land. Flat Rock is now a town, and Two Bears is what they now call the Double Bluff Pass. The caves mentioned are the ones this message is carved in. What else it say?'

Solomon studied the edges of the image where the flash had not quite reached and the petroglyphs fell away into darkness.

'It looks like deVaca made this pledge in the name of someone else,' he pointed at a petroglyph disappearing into shadow and only partially visible. 'See that symbol. I think that denotes deVaca's chief, but without seeing it properly I can't say for sure.'

'Bullshit!' All heads turned as the man in the booth rose from his seat, his newspaper abandoned behind him. He walked over to the counter, people stepping out of his way as he came and stopped in front of Solomon. 'You don't know what those markings say. No one does. The last man alive that could speak the local Suma dialect died over a hunnert and fifty years ago.' He looked Solomon up and down like he was a curiosity in a road-side museum. 'We've had people through here trying to figure out what those markings say, people from all kinds of fancy colleges. Now if they couldn't figure it out why in the hell should anyone believe that you can? I think you're full of it, mister. I don't think you know what this says any more than I do.'

Solomon smiled. 'Well, sir, you are entitled to your opinion. However, as far as the laws relating to gambling in the great state of Texas go, you are not a party to this wager and so your opinion does not matter, legally speaking.' He turned to Rita. 'As the person who took over the bet, the only opinion that matters as to whether I answered the question or not is yours.'

Rita looked over at the man from the booth and nodded. 'You're right,' she said. 'Nobody can prove what these symbols say one way or another so I guess it was kind of a dumb question for me to ask.'

The man from the booth looked pleased, though several members of the crowd did not as they saw their potential winnings slipping away.

'However,' Rita continued, 'seeing as I ain't the kind of person as would cheat a man out of a meal because I went and asked him a dumb question.' She turned back to Solomon and pointed at the menu on the wall. 'Let me know what you want. You just won yourself a wager.'

5

The diner erupted in noise. Men who'd bet on Solomon whooped in victory and those who'd bet against him shook their heads in disbelief.

The man from the booth leaned in and pitched his voice low so it slid beneath the noise. 'You're lucky Rita has such a kind and generous heart,' he said. 'You try this shit anyplace else in West Texas you'd wind up getting shot.' He glared at Rita. 'No wonder this place is on its ass.' He shook his head and marched off back to his booth.

Solomon smiled at Rita and waited for her to notice. 'Friend of yours?'

'Daryl?' Rita shook her head as if even saying his name was wearisome. 'He ain't friends with no one. 'Cept maybe the banks. What you wanna eat?'

'Steak, please, as rare as you dare. Also two eggs, fried and sunnyside, and some home fries if I may.'

She nodded. 'Drink?'

'Ice-water would be fine. Can I ask you a question?'

'Depends. Do I have to buy you another steak dinner if I give you a wrong answer?'

Solomon smiled. 'No, this one's on the house.' He pointed down at the photograph. 'The Indian chief mentioned in this agreement, are you by chance a relative?'

Rita nodded slowly. 'My family name is Treepoint. I think my great-granddaddy changed it in the thirties or forties. I guess *Three Arrows in the Wind* was too much to fit on a cheque.'

'So this land is yours?'

She nodded. 'Government took all the land in 1854 and moved everyone onto reservation ground in the next county, everyone 'cept my family, that is. They stayed put and opened up a trading post so they could make enough money to live. We should have been called *Stubborn as Mules*. Anyways, in 1968, when people finally got around to feeling bad about stealing all our land, the Federal government restored title to us on account of there being a Treepoint on the land continuous for over a hundred years. Which means now it belongs to me, till tomorrow morning leastways.'

Solomon nodded. 'So there never was a Bobby D?'

She shook her head. 'When my granddaddy opened up the gas station he figured white folks were more likely to stop for other white folks so he made him up.' She leaned down and studied the photograph, bringing her head closer to his so that the words she murmured would be heard only by him. 'Does this really say what you said it did?'

Solomon nodded. 'Yes.'

'Can you prove it?'

Solomon twitched his head to the side as more information flooded his mind then shook it. 'No.'

'That's what I thought.'

'For that you'd need to contact a Doctor Andrea Thompson, head of the language unit at the Center for Native American and Indigenous Studies at the University of Colorado. Doctor Thompson and her team recently discovered a new cave system in Colorado near the Arizona border filled with petroglyphs similar to this. They're calling it the Rosetta Stone of the plains because it's filled with petroglyphs from different tribes recording a declaration of peace in several languages. Some, like Sioux, they already know. And some they don't, like Western Suma. But now they can figure it out by comparing it to the languages they do know.'

Rita frowned. 'Then how come these folks ain't come back here to take another look at the cave?'

Solomon shrugged. 'I bet they took plenty of photographs the last time they were here, didn't they?' Rita nodded. 'There you go then. They'll look at those first. The cave in Colorado was only discovered a few months ago and it'll probably take them years to work through the archived material they already have on file.'

Rita nodded again. 'So what you're saying is the only proof you can give me that what you said is true is some academic discovery no one's actually heard of?'

'People in the academic field of Native American studies have heard of it. It's big news for them. You should call the University of Colorado and ask to speak to Doctor Andrea Thompson. She'll confirm everything I just told you.'

Rita smiled sadly. 'I want to believe you, mister, I really do. Only that quarter you said was so rare it was worth at least a hundred bucks.' She slapped her hand down hard on the counter and removed it to reveal two worn quarters. 'I found two more of 'em in the register. So either it's my lucky day and I just happen to have a coupla hundred bucks' worth of rare coins in my cash drawer, or Daryl was right and you're just a smooth-talking grifter looking for an easy meal. Either way what I want you to do is eat your steak and hit the road. We clear?' She held his gaze for a moment then turned and headed back to the kitchen, leaving the two quarters on the counter.

Solomon zeroed in on the dates on the coins, 1976. It didn't matter whether she believed him or not, he'd already secured his meal, which was what he'd come for. Nevertheless, it bothered him that his one lie about the value of the quarter, a lie that should have had no consequence because he knew he wouldn't lose the bet, had now tainted all the truths he'd told her.

'Truth always withers in the shadow of a lie,' he murmured, recalling something from . . . who knew where.

'What's that you say?' the man in the Coors Light T-shirt reappeared at his side, a fistful of dollars in his hand and his face shining with victory.

'Nothing,' Solomon nodded at the money. 'Thanks for the vote of confidence.'

'Nah, man, thank you. Name's Earl,' he bundled his cash into one fist and held out his hand. Solomon took it, shook it then picked up the photograph.

'Say,' Earl said, leaning in close. 'How *do* you know all that stuff? That some kind of a trick or d'ya got one of them, whatya callit, photographic minds or sump'n'?'

'Something like that.' Solomon re-read the message, his mind translating the symbols as his eyes passed over them. 'You a regular here, Earl?'

'I guess. Been coming here for close on twenty years. I run my rig all over the south, delivering pipe mainly. I stop by whenever I'm on the I-10, maybe once a month at the moment. I'll sure miss it if it closes. It's up for auction, you know.'

Solomon nodded. 'So I heard.'

25

'Yep. Damn shame if they close ole Bobby D's. Anyways, just wanted to shake your hand and say if you wanted a ride anyplace east then I'm your man.'

Solomon stretched his legs, still aching from the miles they'd already walked, and thought of the road ahead, his mind providing exact distances to possible destinations:

Corpus Christi 557 miles

Galveston 656 miles

The Gulf of Mexico was maybe two weeks' walk away but he could be there by morning if he caught a lift.

'That would be very kind,' he said. 'When you leaving?'

Rita reappeared with a plate in her hand and clacked it down on the counter in front of Solomon. The steak was almost raw with red juices pooling around the fries and eggs.

'Rare as you dare,' she said, then she picked up the photograph and walked away.

'Man,' Earl said shaking his head. 'That ain't even cooked. You go ahead and take your time eatin' that, you done earned it. I'll go finish my dinner, count my gains and try to figure out the quickest and funnest way to lose it again.' He touched the peak of his cap with a nicotine-stained finger and headed back to his table where a half-eaten basket of chicken wings waited for him.

Solomon cut into the steak, the juices running red around his knife and fork. He put a chunk in his mouth and flavour flooded his tongue, rich and delicious.

Over by the souvenir stand Rita hung the photograph back on the wall. Solomon chewed his steak, the memorized petroglyphs still burning in his mind. He thought of the one showing three arrows and the symbol of a man on horseback and focused on them until the noise of the diner faded and the walls melted away and he sat like a ghost from the future in the middle of a pristine wilderness, before paved roads and power lines, before cars and white streaks in the sky scratched by high-flying planes. He continued to eat and his mind carried him further back to a time before man, when the desert was a field of ice and the slow-moving glaciers carved mesas out of solid stone and crushed boulders to dirt and dust. The land didn't care who owned it, only man cared about that, they cared so much they fought wars over it, spilling blood onto the ground they sought to possess, and carved bargains made with other men into the fabric of the things they sought to own.

'You want dessert?'

Solomon blinked and looked up from his empty plate. He was back in the diner, the endless stretch of the plains replaced by the four thin walls of the cinderblock building.

'A slice of apple pie, if I may. And maybe a cup of coffee.'

'Steady there,' Rita said, sauntering away. 'You're going to bankrupt me with all these outrageous demands.'

He watched her leave and saw her ancestry recorded in the blue-black sway of her crow feather hair, and the lean, sinewy stretch of her limbs, tight and supple like a bow string. She was strong and proud, but also bitter. He could smell disappointment and weariness on her as clear as the bacon grease sizzling on the hot plate in the kitchen. Her ancestor had refused to leave this place, digging in and clinging to deep roots perhaps in the vague hope that his fortunes might one day be restored in some glorious future. And here was his daughter of many times removed, still here, the blood link unbroken over all those years. There was some value in that, though Solomon could not be sure how much without reading the rest of the message on the cave wall, the part the photograph didn't show.

Rita returned with a slice of pie and a mug of black coffee. 'Need anything else?'

Solomon thought about telling her his thoughts but stopped

27

himself. She wouldn't believe him anyway and he could tell she was yearning to leave. She was young enough to start again and there didn't seem to be anything binding her here other than family history. She wore no wedding band, and the photograph of a young girl pinned to the board by the cash register, a mini version of Rita, all smiles despite the gap in her front teeth, was possibly the reason she wanted to go, release herself and her child from the blood ties of tradition that bound them both here. Their people had been nomadic once, like all people had been. Maybe it was time to renew that tradition. So he held onto his thoughts and gave her a smile instead.

'No,' he said. 'I don't need anything else. And thank you for the meal.'

6

The sun was still high in the sky when Solomon climbed into the oven of the big rig's cab. He closed the door and felt the usual anxiety rise up at being confined.

'Mind if I keep the window open?' he said.

'Nope.' Earl settled in his seat and flicked on a small fan clipped to the dashboard. 'Prefer me a breeze to the air-con anyways and it's a damn sight kinder on the fuel.' He twisted the key in the ignition and the truck's engine roared into life. 'Where you headed exactly?'

'East,' Solomon said. 'Galveston, Corpus Christi, Houston, anywhere with ships going to France.'

'What's in France, a lady?'

Solomon opened the flap of his jacket and looked down at the label saying – *This suit was made to treasure for Mr Solomon Creed.*

'The man who made this suit for me, hopefully.'

'Hell, I know a guy in Fort Worth if you need a tailor.'

Solomon let the jacket flap drop. 'I need to see this one specifically,' he said. 'Long story.'

'Well there's a whole lot of road between us and the sea. Happy to hear it if you've a mind to tell.' Earl pulled out of the parking lot and onto the I-10, the roar of the diesels and rumble of tyres drowning out the high-pitched whine of the desert. Solomon looked north across the scrubby plain to a set of red hills that rolled across the distant horizon like an ocean of stone. Somewhere in that rise and fall was a cave with pictures carved on its walls, a natural document sealing a five-hundred-year-old deal. There was nothing else to see. The land was untouched, undeveloped. He thought about Rita with her Irish eyes, queen of all she surveyed, though not for much longer. He shifted in his seat to look back at the diner in the side mirror.

'What's Rita's story?'

'What, you mean like is she married or something?' Earl looked across at Solomon with a smirk on his face. 'You like her, is that it?'

A silver pick-up truck pulled out of the parking lot and joined them on the road.

'No, I mean why's she selling?'

'Money, I guess, same reason as always. Used to be all the trucks had to stop there to gas up but these newer rigs have bigger gas tanks and better fuel consumption so they can hold out for the cheaper gas at the national outlets in the bigger towns. She closed the gas station a while back. I still stop there for lunch but it's more out of habit. Lot of drivers make they own lunch now to cut down on expense. See, most of these southern states are "right to work", which means there's no unions looking out for us and so the big companies get to tell us how they need to cut costs to stay competitive, keep the shareholders happy and all that shit. Bottom line is the working man gets it in the ass like always. I'm on the same rate now I was ten years ago, which wouldn't be so bad if gas and everything else was the same price, only it ain't. Always too much month left at the end of the month. I guess Rita hung in long as she could. She cain't barely make enough from that ole diner to cover her ass.'

'What about the land? The auction notice said there's over three hundred acres.'

'Take a look around, partner. If there's one thing we ain't short of in Texas it's dirt and sunshine. Only value in land like this is if there's oil in it and they already done tested everything between El Paso and the Gulf. I heard they do it with satellites now, don't even need to get they hands dirty. Nah, if there was any oil out here they'd a found it already. I doubt Rita will get more'n a few hunnert bucks an acre for what she got here. Maybe a little more for the diner – eighty, ninety thousand tops if the auction goes well. I hope she gets a good price, I sure do, enough for her and Asha to start off fresh somewhere else leastways.'

'Asha?'

'Rita's little girl.'

'Where's the father?'

'Beats me. I think he lit out before Asha was born. Damn fool. Fine woman, Rita, nice people too.'

Solomon watched the silver pick-up. It was keeping back and out of their dust, maintaining the same distance though it could easily have overtaken the heavier, slower truck. Its windshield was tinted, so he couldn't see who was driving, but he could see a pair of hands resting on the steering wheel and the neatly folded newspaper on the dash.

'The man back there in the diner, the one reading the paper.'

'Daryl Meeks?'

'Yes. What's his story?'

'He's got money behind him, I know that much. Family money. His people was ranchers from way back who found oil on a patch of land that lasted long enough to make 'em rich. Daryl's one of

31

them folks as was born lucky and thinks it makes him special though he ain't never worked a day in his life for the dollars he got in his pocket. He owns property and I heard he's investing in, what you call 'em, renewables, solar panels and wind farms, that kind of thing. I guess he's seen how easy the oil can run out so he's lookin' to the future and something there's plenty of. Maybe he's on to something, I don't know. Don't make him less of an asshole.'

'Any idea why he might be following us?'

Earl leaned forward in his seat and checked his mirror. 'No idea at all. Maybe he cain't see to pass. Let me slow down a little and pull over.'

Earl took his boot off the gas and eased onto the side of the road, his indicator flashing. The pick-up blasted past in a cloud of dust and tore away up the road, its engine whining like a mosquito. The licence plate was *DA RYL 1*.

'Tole you he was an asshole,' Earl said, pulling back onto the road and picking up lost speed. 'You hear that engine? He's got one of those 'lectric cars, hybrid or whatnot. Give me the roar of a diesel any day.'

Solomon watched the pick-up until it melted into the heat-haze. Earl put the radio on and the whine of a slide guitar filled the cab as a smoky-voiced woman sang about love and loss. Solomon took the worn quarter from his pocket and ran it over his fingers, under his palm then back again, thinking about Rita and the land of her ancestors she was getting ready to leave. The song of love and loss segued into one of love and hardship and they passed a sign peppered with bullet holes of various calibres telling them they were leaving Broken Promise. They rumbled across a long, flat bridge over a bone-dry river bed towards a larger, newer billboard on the other side that said '*Welcome to the Lucky Reservation*'. There were no bullet holes in this one.

'There he is again,' Earl pointed beneath the billboard to where the silver pick-up was parked in the shadow.

They drove past and Solomon saw the outline of the driver sitting behind the wheel, his head turning slowly as he watched them pass by.

He sat back in his seat, the quarter rolling over his fingers and thoughts tumbling in his head. Whatever problem Daryl Meeks had with him would only remain one if he stayed here. And this was not his story. He did not need to know its end or help write it.

The coin rolled over his knuckles and under his palm. Over and under. Over and under. They passed another billboard telling them to take the next left for the Lucky Reservation and a sprawling glass-and-terracotta building appeared behind it next to a huge electronic display showing rolling dice, and champagne corks popping, and cards fanning out to show aces. The building was set way back from the road and surrounded by an extensive parking lot with ten-foot, fluorescent-tubed arrows sticking out of it, like the whole place had recently been attacked by giant, neon Indians. The lot had been designed to hold two or three thousand cars and it was more than half full. Lunchtime on a Wednesday and business was booming.

'What do you know about this place?' he said.

'That there's the old reservation. Used to be it was the sorriest scrap of land for five hundred miles in every direction. I guess it still is the reservation. Indian land. Legally proven, which is why they can now run casinos on it. Some kind of loophole in the law.'

They drove past the neon oasis, the distant dots of people disappearing into the perma-darkness of the main building like termites into a hill.

'Decision time,' Earl said nodding at a large road sign ahead

33

of them. 'If I carry on this road I can drop you off maybe a hundred miles shy of Corpus Christi. Or I can take a different route and bring you up nearer Galveston. Don't make any odds to me either way. What's your preference?'

Solomon looked at the sign and saw the miles still to travel. He thought about the pick-up truck, parked in the shadow of the billboard, squatting in the shade, the driver watching him leave, making sure he did. He thought about Rita and how close he'd been to telling her what had come to his mind about the land she was about to sell. He wished he had now. But the diner was behind him, lost in dust and distance, and going back would only add miles to the ones he still had to travel. He had no reason to go back. None at all.

The quarter continued to travel across the knuckles of his hand – over and under, over and under. Then he stopped and flicked it into the air, watching it spin and deciding in his head that if it came down tails he would continue to Galveston and if it was heads he would go to Corpus Christi. He caught the quarter, smacked it down then lifted his hand so he could see which way it had fallen. Tails.

'So which is it?' Earl said.

Solomon palmed the coin and slipped it into his pocket. 'Just drop me off anywhere.'

'Here? You sure?'

'Not really.'

Earl eased over to the side of the road and came to a halt in a cloud of fine grit. Solomon opened his door and felt the relief of being released from the tin can of the cab.

'You sure I can't take you a little further?' Earl said. 'It's no bother and I feel like I owe you.'

'No. Thank you. And thank you for the ride.' He went to close the door then paused. 'Actually, there is one thing.'

'Name it.'

'That roll of cash you made betting on me. Could you maybe spare a dollar of it?'

Earl shook his head and smiled. 'Son, I made so much on that crazy bet I'll give you twenty.'

7

The sun was starting to slide down the sky like butter in a hot
pan by the time the lunchtime crowd dwindled and Rita finally
had a moment to herself. She stood spooning coffee into the
machine, thinking that this was about the last time she would
ever do it, the last time she would wait for the school bus to
drop Asha off outside, the last time a member of her tribe
would walk across this scrap of land and call themselves the
owner.

She set the coffee brewing then sat at the counter, stretching
her back and rolling her feet to get the blood flowing. Just a few
more hours and she would close forever. She had told the regulars she would not be running the evening shift, too much to do,
too much to sort out. So this was it, her final shift, possibly ever.
She wouldn't miss standing up all day or the smell of grease she
could never entirely wash from her hair.

She looked out at the parking lot where the school bus would
be pulling up any minute now. Her car was parked right outside,
a 1986 Buick Electra station wagon with over two hundred thousand miles on the clock, its hood lifting up like a dog sniffing

the air because everything she owned in the world was packed inside and pushing down hard on the back axle. Thirty-four years of a life squeezed into the back of a station wagon. She'd had one of the regulars check it over in exchange for an extra slice of pie and he'd said it was good for another two hundred thousand miles providing she didn't drive it too hard.

As soon as the place was sold she was going to get in that car, turn on a top forty station and hit the road. She didn't plan on stopping until they came across somewhere green and healthy and full of life. Somewhere she could put down roots and watch her daughter grow. Somewhere the exact opposite of Broken Promise, Texas. All she needed was a little stake money. The guide price on the diner and attached land was fifty thousand dollars, though the auctioneer said it might make more.

Fifty thousand dollars.

Not much for her ancestral homeland. Twice that amount would be better. Some of the regulars said they'd happily give her that just to keep everything exactly the way it was, but talk was cheap and, sweet as they were, she couldn't spend kind words and compliments. They were all of them dreamers, staking their futures on the lottery, or scratch cards, or on making one big score somewhere down the line. She'd been doing the same thing for long enough, hoping the tourists might start coming back, or some big oil company would come along and buy her out so they could re-open the gas station. Her father had similar dreams. After they'd built the casino on the old reservation lands he'd tried to have their land officially designated as ancestral land. She'd found the rejection letter when putting all the legal documents together for the auction.

'Indian ancestral lands must be historically proven and ratified by either Federal decree or by other legally recognized sovereign power.'

Rita looked across at the photograph of the petroglyphs. The stranger had said it recorded an agreement between her ancestor and Cabeza deVaca, an envoy of the King of Spain. A sovereign power. Then again he'd also claimed a coin worth twenty-five cents was worth a hundred bucks, so his word wasn't exactly scripture. But if there *was* any truth in what he said, anything at all, it would certainly be worth knowing, even if just to tell the auctioneer so he could maybe boost the price a little.

She pulled her phone from her pocket, opened a browser and typed in *Rosetta of the Plains*, the weak data signal creating a dramatic pause before the results came back.

'Damn,' Rita whispered when she saw how many results came back. There were pages of them. Pictures too. She clicked on one and the slow internet made her wait again while a photograph slowly sharpened on the screen to reveal a large cave covered with thousands of petroglyphs. A blonde woman with cornflower-blue eyes stood smiling in the foreground, the caption beneath identifying her as Doctor Andrea Thompson from the University of Colorado.

'Damn,' Rita muttered again. It was the name the stranger had given her, the person he said could prove what he'd claimed was true.

She Googled the University of Colorado, tapping her foot impatiently while the results loaded, then hit the top link and continued to tap while the home page loaded. She scrolled down, searching for a contact number for Doctor Thompson. The bell above the door jangled and she looked up expecting to see her daughter. It wasn't Asha. It was Daryl Meeks, carrying a briefcase and accompanied by a man in a grey suit that had 'attorney' written all over it.

'Hey Reet, got a minute?' Meeks said, gesturing towards his favourite booth.

'Sure,' Rita said. She got up, feeling the pain of the day in her feet, and walked over to join them, closing her phone as she went so Meeks wouldn't see what she'd been looking at.

8

Meeks smiled at Rita as she sat down and it made her feel uncomfortable. She couldn't remember ever seeing him smile before and his face looked like it was hurting from the effort.

'Got something of a proposition for ya.' He laid the briefcase on the table between them and ran his hands over the top of it.

Rita looked at the briefcase then up at the man in the grey suit.

'This here's Nate Prime,' Meeks said. 'He's what you might call a business associate. Helps me out from time to time with the legal side of my business. Purchases and leases and whatnot.'

Rita nodded. 'A lawyer.'

The man in the suit smiled and displayed a row of shark white teeth. 'Estates attorney,' he said, handing Rita a card which read:

Prime Estates
Nathaniel Prime – Partner at Law

Rita put the card down on the table next to her phone. 'What's the proposition?'

Meeks's smile widened. 'Well, as you may know, I've expressed an interest in purchasing your little spread here.'

Rita nodded. 'You and a few others.' She nodded at the briefcase. 'Is your interest in here?'

The smile continued to split Meeks's face. 'Well now, you just get right to the point, don't ya?'

'I got coffees to refill and trash that won't take itself out, so if you want to make me an offer, let's hear it.'

The smile fell a little. Rita wasn't sure if it was because Meeks's face wasn't used to it or he didn't like being told what to do, especially by a woman. Either way she didn't care.

'You want to sell,' Meeks said. 'I want to buy. Now we could wait till morning and see what happens at the auction. Maybe you'll get a good price, maybe not. What I'm proposing is to take the guesswork out for everyone and make what we call a pre-emptive offer.'

'How much?'

'Nate here has already drawn up the paperwork.' The man in the grey suit reached into his pocket and pulled out an envelope. 'So if we can agree a price all I'd need is your signature and we can shake hands and avoid the uncertainty of an auction.'

'How much?' Rita repeated.

'I believe the guide price for this here lot has been set at fifty thousand dollars.'

Rita shrugged. 'Just a guide.'

'Ms Treepoint,' the lawyer leaned in, picking up the conversation. 'I don't know how much experience you have of property auctions. Truth is, the guide price is exactly as stated, only a guide. Now I've been to hundreds of auctions, thousands even, and seen the hammer drop on final bids of a few hundred thousand dollars on properties with guides of a million or more.'

'I bet you've seen things go for twice and three times as much too.'

The lawyer held his smile. 'As a general rule the guide price sits about right. A good auctioneer will start things a little below the guide and hope to drive the price so it finishes somewhere above it. Sometimes it works. Sometimes it don't. Now I would say the guide on this property is a shade on the optimistic side, given the current market and the fact you got an old gas station out there to contend with. Lot of extra expense to deal with ground decontamination, decommissioning the old tanks and what have you. Hell, there's state law a foot thick needs to be satisfied on that kind of thing, and that's bound to put off a whole bunch of potential buyers.'

Rita looked back at Daryl Meeks. 'But not you?'

Meeks opened his hands. 'What can I say, I like a challenge, and I'm kind of attached to this old place, all of which is to say that I might be prepared to take it on, *if* the price is right.'

Rita stared at him. He was a real type, one of those good ole boys who came in here and liked to hear his own voice and boss her around because she wore a waitress uniform.

'I've asked you three times now,' she said, trying to keep the annoyance out of her voice. 'So unless you're going to tell me the figure you got in mind we're done here, my daughter's going to be back from school any minute and I need to fix her some dinner.'

Meeks lifted the lid of the briefcase. It was full of money, neatly bound crisp notes fresh from the bank. Fifties in thousand-dollar bundles. Sixty in all.

'Sixty thousand cash,' Meeks said, keeping his voice low and the briefcase angled away from the room so only Rita could see it. 'You can buy your daughter a whole lot of fancy dinners with that kind of money.'

Rita stared at the bundles of notes. It didn't look like much, just a few stacks of paper, but if she said the number in her head it seemed much bigger. Sixty thousand dollars would be enough to put a down payment on a decent place and leave a little for living. It was their ticket out of here. A new beginning. Lying on the table in front of her.

'Now that there's a fair offer,' Meeks said. 'More'n fair. And all you have to do is sign these papers and it's yours.'

The lawyer placed the envelope down on the table next to Rita's phone just as it buzzed and the screen lit up with a text message. The website for the University of Colorado was clearly visible behind it. Rita snatched up the phone, hoping Meeks hadn't seen. The message was from one of her regulars.

> *Good Luck with the sale. Sorry I couldn't make it for one last bowl of chilli. Keep in touch. RoadHog <3*

'Heading to college?' Meeks said.

Rita felt her face flush. He *had* seen the website on her phone. So he knew she'd been looking and he'd also know why. She looked at the case full of money, more money than she'd cleared in the last three years of constant work and worry. All she had to do was sign a piece of paper and it would be hers.

'Why now?' she said. 'Why show up with a case full of cash the evening before the auction? The notice went up over a month ago.'

Meeks shrugged. 'I needed some time to consider my offer. Do some background checks, draw up the paperwork.'

'But why not make the offer earlier when you stopped by for lunch? What changed?'

'Nothing. Nothing changed.'

The lawyer leaned in. 'An offer's only an offer until the cheque clears.' He smiled and it reminded Rita of the tiles in the men's room. 'This here's not an offer, it's a serious declaration of intent to buy. Sign the papers and you won't have to wait for anything. You can be gone whenever you want. Off to your new life and with a comfortable amount of cash in your pocket.'

Rita looked back down at the cash. 'That won't fit in my pocket.'

'Keep the case,' Meeks said, a hard edge creeping into his voice.

'Can I think about it?'

'No.' Meeks brought his hand down flat on the table and a few heads turned in their direction. He waited until they'd turned back again before continuing in a low voice. 'This here's a one-time offer. You accept it right now or I walk away and we'll just have to see what happens tomorrow at the auction.'

Rita saw the stiffness around his jaw that showed he was clenching it. He was losing patience and finding it hard to hide it.

'You know I get salesmen in here all the time trying to get me to buy all kinda things – water coolers, insurance, new filters for the fryers. They always got some special discount, some deal they can only give me if I sign there and then. So I'm wondering to myself, is that why you showed up with this money right now? Dazzle the poor brown girl with a whole pile of silver then threaten to take it away if she don't sign something right now. Let me tell you something, Daryl.' She leaned in and spoke low. 'I ain't some trembling squaw can be bought for a blanket and a bucket of beads.'

The bell jangled again and Rita turned to see her daughter walk in, her school bag sagging heavy on her back.

'Go sit at the counter,' Rita said. 'I'll be with you in a minute.'

Asha looked at Meeks and the lawyer in the suit then moved away, passing through the hatch in the counter and heading for the iced-water jug.

'Think about your daughter,' Meeks whispered. 'Think about Asha and what this money could mean for her. How old is she

44

now, seven? Eight?' He reached across the table, picked up Rita's phone and pressed a button to make the screen light up with the website for the University of Colorado. 'You want to risk all that to go chasing something some roadside conman said about what *might* be written in those caves?'

'Give me my phone back.'

Meeks smiled. 'Sure.' He laid it down on the table next to the envelope. 'Listen, Rita. You want to leave this place. I'm just offering you the ticket. Now, you can sell to me right now for what is a very fair price, or you can sell it to me tomorrow for who knows what – maybe more, probably less.'

Meeks sat back and folded his arms like he thought he was holding all the cards. People like him always did. People with money. They always thought everything can be bought. But he was wrong.

'You can't buy this place if I withdraw it from auction,' Rita said.

She saw something harden in his eyes. 'Now why would you go and do a thing like that?'

She shrugged. 'I don't know. Maybe this place is undervalued. Maybe you think that too, which is why you showed up with your case full of cash and your cheap sales routine. Either way, my response to your offer is "No". Now if you gentlemen ain't planning on ordering anything you can hit the road, because I'm fixing to close up pretty soon. Careful the door don't hit you on the ass on your way out.'

9

Solomon stepped into the casino and experienced the same kind of nausea he felt whenever he got into a car. He stood for a moment, adjusting to the barn-like room, the beep and chatter of the slot machines, the smell of greed and overstimulation, of hickory smoke barbecue sauce, of adrenaline and sweat and low-level depression. It was a twilight place, unnatural, disconnected, the only brightness coming from gaudy light displays and the frantic flicker and shimmer of slot machines hypnotizing the passing people and drawing them in like moths. It seemed extraordinary to him that anyone would voluntarily spend time in this plastic environment when outside the sky was so big and boundless, and the air so rich and fresh. He searched his memory for some recollection of ever having been in a place like this before but drew a blank. If he had he couldn't remember.

He moved further into the room past a circular bar with low lighting that made it feel forever midnight. The clientele clustered around it reminded Solomon of the people back in the diner: same clothes, same body types. Only the men here were sipping cocktails through tiny straws or sucking the foam off cold beers

46

while pretty women in cocktail dresses pressed close and laughed at whatever they said.

He headed deeper into the casino, past the roulette wheels, the craps and the blackjack tables, the poker huddles, the blue baize tables like bright pools of water and the players like cattle come to drink. He did a full circle of the room, his mind shimmering with information about each game being played, the rules, the ways to cheat and the risks associated. He also read the people, the drunk and reckless gamblers and the cautious ones too. But mostly he looked at the dealers.

He finished his circuit, swapped his twenty-dollar bill at a cashier's window for four five-dollar chips then headed back to the blackjack pit, riffling them in his hand, the hard plastic click lost amid the constant chatter of slot machines. The percentage play was to take things steady, bet small, risk little, and increase his meagre stake steadily. But even with the absence of clocks in this timeless place Solomon could feel time passing. He should be heading to Galveston right now, thirty or forty miles further up the road. But Rita had done him a favour. She could easily have blown his story about the bicentennial quarter and kicked him out, disgraced and hungry. But she hadn't and he wanted to pay her back, not just for the meal but also for her kindness. And for that he wanted to give her something of real value if he could. He figured if he could finish here quickly and head back up the road to the diner before evening he could catch another ride east and easily make up what time he'd lost. He sat down at a five-dollar-minimum-bet table, the lowest he could go, and placed his stack of four chips in front of him. He had twenty dollars and a plan but not a great deal of time. He would have to take risks. Four chips. Four chances.

The dealer gathered the cards and chips from the previous deal and smiled at him. 'Hi,' he said, 'my name's Ryan. Welcome to the game, sir.'

47

His words were bright but he had a slight tightness in his shoulders and a tiny trace of grime around the neck of his white shirt, suggesting he was at the end of a long shift. One of the cardinal rules of gambling that had popped into Solomon's head as he'd toured the room was that you should never gamble when tired or drunk. Dealers never drank, but they did get tired. This was partly why Solomon had chosen this table, though there were other reasons. He placed one of his five-dollar chips on the betting circle in front of him and studied the other gamblers.

There were five more players at the table, four men in check shirts and baseball caps who could have come here straight from the diner, and a woman, skeletal thin with watchful eyes. She had the most chips in front of her and she played with a sharp, quiet, unblinking focus.

The dealer finished the deal. Solomon had a Five of Hearts and a Jack of Spades. Fifteen.

The dealer had a Seven of Clubs showing and another card lying face down.

One by one the men all hit and busted out but the woman drew a Nine of Diamonds, to add to a Queen, making her hand worth nineteen. Solomon also hit and got a Seven of Clubs. Twenty-two. Bust.

The dealer turned over his other card. Four of Diamonds. Added to the seven it gave him eleven. He took another card and got a Queen. Twenty-one. House wins.

One of the men rose from his seat and dragged his few remaining chips across the baize towards his bulging stomach. 'I ain't tipping you,' he said to the dealer. 'Not with the bullshit cards you been giving me.'

'Better luck next time, sir,' the dealer replied, his professional veneer as smooth as the coating on the cards he was collecting. 'You have a good day now.'

The man grunted and ambled away, cupping his chips in his large hands like he was carrying water across the desert.

Solomon lost the next hand but the woman won with a five-card eighteen that helped to draw more cards from the deck than a usual deal. Solomon had now seen more than a full deck's worth of cards dealt. He waited for the dealer to shuffle the shoe but he didn't, he let it ride. Maybe he was tired, maybe he was just lazy. Either way this was the time to take a risk. Solomon looked at his two chips, ten dollars in total and, apart from the worn quarter in his pocket, all the money he had in the world. He didn't have the time or resources to play it cautious and, besides, if he lost everything on the flop of a card there was another way he might repay Rita for her kindness.

He pushed the two five-dollar chips into the betting circle.

And waited for his cards.

10

'What was all that about?' Asha fixed Rita with her single-raised-eyebrow look, the one that made her seem about twenty years older than she was.

'Ah, just Daryl Meeks waving his money around as usual. What you want for supper? Bear in mind this'll be your last chance of free food for a while so knock yourself out.'

'Anything I want?'

Rita waved at the board. 'If it's up there and we got any of it left it's yours.'

'Cool. I'll have a . . . cheeseburger. Fries. Chocolate shake. And vanilla ice cream on hot waffles to finish.'

Rita smiled. 'Good choice, though we're out of ice cream and waffles.'

She passed through the counter hatch and into the kitchen, threw a beef patty on the grill and dropped some fries in oil. The cook had already gone; she'd let him off early and they'd exchanged an awkward hug and half-hearted words about keeping in touch. It all seemed unreal somehow, the notion that this time tomorrow all of this might belong to someone else and she and Asha would be heading down the road to who knew where.

She flipped the burger, shook the fries and thought about Meeks's offer. Now she was no longer facing him and his smooth lawyer friend she didn't feel so pressured or hostile to the idea of selling to him. She looked out at Asha, hunched over the counter and frowning at some game on her tablet, looking every inch an eight-year-old kid again. Why hadn't she taken the deal? It was a lot of money. If it had been anyone other than Meeks she might have done. It was only his bullshit, greasy salesman routine that had made her act defensive, that and the way he had reacted so coldly when he'd seen what was on her phone.

She pulled it from her pocket, the website for the University of Colorado still displayed on it. Why would he react at all unless he recognized the website and knew why she might be looking it up? But if Meeks *had* checked out the stranger's story and discovered the land was more valuable, then so could she. She scrolled down, found the general number for the university switchboard and dialled it. The phone beeped in her ear and she checked the signal. Nothing.

'Shit!'

'I heard that,' Asha said without taking her eyes from her screen.

'Well you shouldn't be listening.'

She moved out of the kitchen and grabbed the old payphone from the wall by the countertop, keeping her eye on the burger and fries through the kitchen door as she dialled the number for the University of Colorado. The phone connected and an automated switchboard gave her a list of options. She chose one for the Center for Native American and Indigenous Studies and holding music started playing in her ear. She ducked quickly back into the kitchen, flipped the burger and dropped a square of

51

Monterey Jack on it and was back on the phone again just as it connected and she finally got through to a human.

'You've reached the CNAIS, can I help you?' The woman's voice sounded old and dry and reminded Rita of her old kindergarten teacher who'd spent most of her time telling the kids not to slouch.

'Yes, could you put me through to a Doctor Andrea Thompson, please.' Rita found herself standing up straight as she spoke.

'Doctor Thompson is working from home today. I can put you through to her office extension so you can leave a message if you like?'

'I really need to talk to her now if that's possible.'

'I'm afraid not. Let me put you through to her office.'

'No wait, do you have another nu—'

The line cut out and Rita listened to static and clicks as she was redirected. At least if this Doctor Thompson wasn't in the office it meant Daryl Meeks couldn't have talked to her either. So he'd been taking a risk, offering her ten thousand dollars above guide price to take it off the table. Though ten thousand dollars was hardly a risk for someone with his money.

'Hi, you've reached Andrea Thompson,' a soft voice purred in Rita's ear. 'I'm sorry I can't answer the phone right now. Please leave your name, number and the purpose of your call and I'll get back to you as soon as I can.'

There was a click and a beep.

'Hi, yes. My name is Rita Treepoint. My people are Western Suma and I was hoping you might look at some petroglyphs I have on my land. I can send you pictures but I think someone from your department came out here maybe ten years back and took some then, so you should have them in an archive or something. Anyway, the name of the place is Broken Promise, West Texas, and my number is 555-89703. If you could get back to me

52

urgently I would really appreciate it. The thing is, this land is due to be sold tomorrow morning and I need to know if the message changes the value. I'll explain when you call back. Thank you.'

She hung up and stared at the phone. If she could somehow get in contact with Doctor Thompson tonight and confirm the message on the cave wall was a genuine treaty between her ancestors and Cabeza deVaca then it would be worth cancelling the auction and re-listing it. Federally recognized Indian ancestral lands, with all the potentially lucrative things that came with it concerning gaming licences and possible casino development, would quadruple the value. More. She could always cancel the auction until after she'd spoken to her, though doing so this late would incur a penalty of two percent of the guide price plus tax – roughly twelve hundred dollars she didn't have. She needed to talk to her tonight.

She went back in the kitchen, swept the burger into a bun, drained the fries and tipped them onto a plate and took it out to her daughter.

'Borrow this for a second,' Rita swapped Asha's tablet for the burger and fries.

'You want to play Minecraft?'

'No, wiseass, I want to use the camera, it's way better than the one on my phone.'

'Everything in the world is better than your phone,' Asha murmured, squirting ketchup into the bun and taking a big bite.

'That's because I'm an awesome mom who buys her daughter iPads instead of getting herself a fancy new phone.' She held up the tablet and framed the photograph of the petroglyphs, making sure it filled the frame and was in focus before she took a picture. She looked at the image on the tablet. It was as good as the original, which meant it looked sun-faded and the edges fell away to darkness where the flash hadn't quite reached. She'd always intended to go out to the caves one day to take better pictures. Now she had no days left. It would have to do.

'How do I email this to someone?'

'I can do it,' Asha said. 'Who d'ya wanna send it to?'

Rita handed the tablet back and looked through the University of Colorado website on her phone for an email address for Doctor Thompson.

'All the emails listed here are general enquiry ones for different departments. I need to send it to someone specific.'

'Lemme see.' Asha took her phone and laid it on the counter next to the tablet, her brow creased in concentration as her nimble fingers navigated the site. Rita felt an almost painful surge of love as she watched her. She never got tired of looking at her daughter. She was luminous and ever changing and beautiful, like staring into a fire at night.

'They don't have email addresses,' Asha said, her fingers still searching the site. 'Except for this one I found for the Dean. It's just his name in small writing so I guess they'll all be like that. Who d'you want to send this to again?'

'Doctor Andrea Thompson.'

'OK. I'll bet they probably drop the doctor bit to keep it short.' She opened up an email with the photo already attached and addressed it to andreathompson@coloradoU.com.

'What's the subject?'

'Let me type it.' Rita took the tablet back and typed 'WESTERN SUMA PETROGLYPHS' in the subject line and added 'URGENT'.

'I think you should add six or seven exclamation points,' Asha said, 'and maybe a shocked face emoji.'

Rita smiled. 'Let's not overdo it.'

She clicked on the message space and typed: 'I left a message on your voicemail about the attached. Please get back to me as soon as you can. Regards, Rita Treepoint.' She added her cellphone number and also the number of the payphone in the diner in case the signal dropped out, then she read it all through and hit *Return.*

'If it pings back we know we got the address wrong,' Asha said.

They watched the tablet. Waited. Nothing happened.

'Who's Doctor Thompson?' Asha asked.

Rita pulled out a stool and sat down. 'Someone who might tell us what the writing in Three Arrow Cave says.'

'Cool!' Asha frowned. 'But I thought no one could speak that language any more.'

'Apparently they figured it out.'

Asha's eyes went wide. 'What if it's, like, some kind of treasure map and we find a ton of gold and don't have to sell up after all?'

Rita smiled then frowned. 'Don't you want to get out of here?'

Asha shrugged. 'I guess. There's not much to do here. Only thing that bothers me about going is . . .' she paused and chewed her lip.

'Your dad,' Rita said. 'You think if we stick around maybe he might swing through again one day?'

Asha nodded.

'Honey, I don't think that's gonna happen.'

'You don't know that. Maybe he will come back.'

'Or maybe he won't. Maybe he got a new family. Maybe he's in prison. Or maybe . . .'

'Maybe he's dead?' Asha whispered, her eyes clouding a little.

Rita felt an ache deep in the centre of her body, the pain of having to tell an ugly truth to someone you loved.

'Honey, it's fine to have these ideas about your dad, who he might be and what it would be like if he came back. Every kid has them, even ones who have their parents around imagine they might really be the kids of kings and stuff like that. But they're

55

just fantasies and you can't go hanging your life on them. When I told your dad I was expecting you, he *promised* me he'd look after us. Said he had all kinds of plans about fixing this place up and making a go of it together, though he never told me what those plans were. Then one night he headed out and never came back. I thought he might show up again once you arrived, that he might've worked out whatever crap was going on in his head made him take off like that. But that was eight years ago now. And there comes a point when you just got to let things go. We can't keep waiting around here forever, hoping he still might show up one day. We need to move on with our lives. I need to move on.'

Asha took a deep breath, nodded then looked down at the tablet. 'That email didn't ping back. Let's hope all those exclamation points did the trick and she writes back. Maybe there will be treasure in those caves after all.'

'Whatever it says, they'll always be part of our history, our story.' Rita looked around at the few customers still lingering, a new idea forming in her mind. 'What say we close up and hike out to the cave one last time?'

Asha smiled. 'I'd like that.'

'Me too. Finish your burger and go grab some warm clothes. And bring your tablet, I want to make sure we have some proper pictures of the cave. That way we'll always have it with us, wherever we end up.'

11

The last few customers were reluctant to leave, nursing their cups of coffee and bowls of chilli like condemned men dragging out final meals.

'End of an era,' one trucker said as Rita all but pushed him out of the door. 'Won't be the same once this place closes.'

'Ah, they'll probably turn it into a McDonald's or a Starbucks and you'll forget I was ever here,' Rita said, touched by his sentiments but equally eager to get him gone so she and Asha could set off for the caves while there was still some daylight left.

She closed the door for the last time, twisted the key in the lock and turned the sign round so it said 'CLOSED'. She listened to the tinkling sound of the bell melting away in the greasy air then took a deep breath and turned to Asha. 'All set?'

Asha held up a rucksack. 'But if I get bit by a snake and die out there I'll haunt you, like, forever.'

Rita smiled. 'I'd like that. Just stomp a little as you walk to drive the snakes away. You'll be fine.'

Evening was starting to bruise the western sky as they went out through the kitchen delivery door, the sun almost gone and the rapidly darkening land rolling away from them like a petrified ocean. They left the compacted dirt and cracked concrete of the parking lot and crunched onto the soft sand and grit of the prairie. Somewhere close by a tall flowering tobacco began to fill the warm evening air with its sweet, narcotic perfume and it struck Rita how, whenever she managed to escape the stink of chicken and bacon grease, she loved the smell of the land. There was something familiar and comforting about it, timeless and pure.

When she was Asha's age she'd thought she had some kind of special connection to the earth because of her heritage. But the older she got, and the more people she met, the more she realized it was something universal, something as old as the land itself, and that what she was experiencing when she breathed in the smells of tobacco and creosote, and felt the soft, warm wind on her skin, and the crunch of the dry earth beneath her feet, was simply a recognition of what we all were. Creatures of nature. Part of it, and not apart. Her ancestors had understood this truth. The only god they ever worshipped was the sun. It was one of the few symbols carved on the cave wall that everyone had agreed on.

They walked in silence for a long time, just the faint crunch of their footsteps breaking the rapidly deepening gloom.

'When was the last time we came out here?' she asked, trying to remember.

'It's been a while,' Asha said. 'I think I was seven maybe?'

'Think you'll miss it?'

Asha went silent for a moment before answering. 'I'm not sure. It's hard to imagine missing a place when you're still there. I don't even know where we're going. It might be somewhere awesome and I won't miss anything. Or it might be a dump and I'll miss everything and cry myself to sleep each night.'

58

'Way to go with the guilt trip.'

Asha smiled. 'What about you? Will you miss anything?'

Rita shook her head. 'I don't think I'll miss it at all. The best thing about this place is you and I'm taking you with me.'

The night was deepening now, the sun long gone and the sky becoming as dark as the land beneath. Rita could see Venus, rising to the east, brighter than anything in the sky, and used it to correct their route a little. She could see the rise up ahead, and from there she would be able to see all the way clear to the horizon and the jagged rock which marked the entrance to the cave. Asha saw it too and scampered ahead, remembering the way from the last time. She reached the top of the rise then stopped suddenly, her body tensing in a way that made Rita's heart race. Rita moved faster and joined Asha on top of the rise. Then she saw what it was that had made her freeze.

A faint glow.

Still some way distant and low to the ground.

It was by the entrance to the caves. A fire.

Someone was there.

12

Rita dropped to the ground and pulled Asha down with her so their outlines couldn't be seen against the sky.

She stared ahead at the flickering glow reflecting off the burnt earth. Rita was twitchy about fires. A few years earlier a bunch of hippies had camped out near the caves and lit a huge fire while out of their heads on mescaline and peyote. The resulting wildfire had come pretty close to the diner before the fire department managed to get it under control. Everything had smelled of smoke for months after and the desert had been left blackened and scorched. The last thing she needed was a fire the night before the auction. Who in their right mind would buy a piece of burning land? Whoever was up ahead was not only trespassing, they were also putting her property and therefore her daughter's future at risk. And that pissed her off.

'Stay here,' she whispered through tight teeth. 'I'll go check it out.'

'No way,' Asha hissed. 'I'm not staying here on my own.'

'Honey, I need to check the fire is safe is all.'

'Then I'll come with you.'

Rita looked at her daughter and saw the whites of her wide open eyes standing out against the night. It was easy to forget sometimes, with how sassy she was, that she was still only eight years old.

'OK, but stay behind me and move slow. And don't make any sound 'cause noise travels at night. If I hold my hand up for any reason you stop and you hit the deck and you stay there till I tell you to get up again. Clear?'

Asha nodded. Rita turned back to the distant glow and started moving towards it, picking her way carefully along the barely visible trail, listening ahead for any sounds. After a few minutes of careful progress she heard the faint crackle of fire and the pop of coal tar sap in the burning creosote branches. She listened hard but couldn't hear anything else. No voices. No movement. Nothing.

She moved closer and stopped just short of the caves at a spot where the ground dipped. When Asha joined her Rita leaned in and put her mouth to her daughter's ear.

'I'm going to take a look,' she whispered. 'Stay out of sight and listen out.' She pulled her phone from her pocket and pressed it into Asha's hands, keeping the screen covered so it didn't leak light. 'If it sounds like I'm having any trouble, you dial the Sheriff's office and tell them where we are, OK? But keep quiet and out of sight. Move away before you make the call.'

Rita leaned back and saw her daughter's eyes had grown wide again. She smiled to reassure her. 'It's probably just some kids playing at cowboys. I'll take a peek, make sure the fire's safe, then come right back, OK?'

Asha nodded and Rita kissed the tips of her fingers, touched them to her daughter's forehead then turned and crawled forward on all fours to the edge of the rise, peering into the shallow gulch where the entrance to the cave was hidden.

The fire was bright to Rita's night-saturated eyes and she had to squint against the flickering glare of it. It had been built in the dead centre of the dip and the ground around had been swept to stop the flames from spreading. The person who had built it clearly knew what they were doing, though whoever it was, there was no sign of them now.

Rita blinked a few times to adjust her eyes and studied the ground. She could make out boot marks in the dirt where the dry straw had been kicked into the centre where the fire now burned. There was also a small pile of dried cactus and a neat stack of mesquite branches lying next to it. Two of the sticks had been laid with their ends in the flames, like someone had been toasting marshmallows and dropped them in the fire. There was nothing else: no backpack, no bedroll, no water jug or provisions of any kind.

She looked across at the entrance to the cave system, a large boulder resting against a smaller one. Whoever had lit the fire had to be inside. She watched for a moment, looking for any flicker of light or movement in the triangle of darkness that formed the entrance, wondering what to do. She should leave, that's what, go back to Asha and make their way back to the diner. There was still stuff to pack and they had a long day ahead of them tomorrow, driving off to who knew where. The fire was too small and too well set to be dangerous and there was no wind to carry burning embers out onto the wider land. They could always come back here after the auction and get some photos of the cave then. That's what they'd do. They'd come back tomorrow.

Rita tensed her arms ready to crawl back away from the rim of the hollow when she saw something. A faint flicker in the dark triangle between the two boulders. Someone *was* in the cave, and they were coming out.

She dropped lower, pressing herself into the ground, and

watched the flickering orange get brighter in the black. A small flame appeared between the boulders, curling around the end of a burned stick. Then a tall, thin man appeared and held the flickering branch high over his head to show his face. It was the stranger from earlier.

'Come and look,' Solomon said, looking straight at Rita though she knew she was hidden. 'Bring your daughter. She should see it too.'

He dropped his burning stick into the heart of the fire and took out the two longer ones. He speared a couple of pieces of the broken, dried cactus with the burning points, turned them to spread the flames then headed back to the gap in the boulders, the makeshift torches throwing light all around him as he disappeared back into the cave.

63

13

Solomon waited, listening to the whisper of a low, tense conversation taking place outside the cave. It had not been hard to find; all the trails north of the diner had led here, the traffic of previous sightseers compacting the dirt and pointing the way. His plan had been to read the message on the wall and head to the diner if what it said was in any way beneficial to Rita, but turn around and head back east if it was not. Now she was here he would have to tell her regardless. Outside the whispering stopped and was replaced by the crunch of footsteps, then a bright, blue-white light shone into his face and blinded him.

'Flaming torches is all very dramatic,' Rita said from behind the blue light, 'but a Maglite is less smoky. Now d'you mind telling me what in the hell you're doing out here sneaking around at night and lighting fires on private land?'

Solomon held his hand up to shield the glare and could just about see the shape of her behind the dazzling light, a miniature version standing next to her – Rita's daughter, he assumed.

'I was hoping to repay your earlier kindness,' Solomon replied.

'I came to read the rest of the message, the part not shown on the photograph, to see if it might be of value to you.'

The beam shifted slightly, out of Solomon's face. 'And is it?'

Solomon shrugged. 'I haven't actually seen it yet. These fire-brands, dramatic as they are, don't have much in the way of range. So far I've only managed to search the first few chambers and I imagine the cave with the petroglyphs will be much deeper. Why don't you show me, lead the way with your painfully bright torch and I'll tell you what it says.'

Rita hesitated and Solomon saw her turn to her daughter, and a silent conversation took place in shrugs and head shakes. Solomon could sense her hesitation but he could also feel the desire to know coming off her like heat.

She turned back to Solomon and pointed the torch beam down the main tunnel that led to the lower chambers. 'You first,' she said. 'And I've got a gun in my pocket, so don't get cute.'

Solomon smiled and stuck the points of his two burning sticks into the dirt floor, snuffing out the flames. 'You haven't got a gun,' he said, and turned and walked away, heading down into the system of caves.

'You don't know that,' Rita said, following and pulling Asha along behind her.

'Yes I do.'

'How?'

'Because if you had a gun it would be in your hand by now,' he ducked through a low arch and stepped into the darkness beyond.

Rita picked up the pace, shining her torch after him to light the way and make sure he wasn't getting ready to try something. Solomon stood with his back to the light, pointing at the two tunnels in front.

'Which way?'

'The one on the right,' Rita replied, and he was gone again before she'd finished answering.

'You know this guy?' Asha whispered.

'He was in the diner earlier, spinning some yarn about how he could read the writing in the cave.'

'Really? But I thought no one could read Suma?'

'They can't, he's just some conman is all.'

Solomon reappeared from the darkness, so suddenly it made Rita stop and stumble backwards, her arm thrown out to the side to protect Asha.

'It's Asha, isn't it?' Solomon said, addressing the girl. Asha nodded. 'I'm Solomon and I assure you that I am not a conman, but the fact that your mother thinks I am is the reason I came back.'

'You told me a plain old quarter was worth a hundred bucks.'

'That's not correct,' Solomon said, turning away and heading back into the tunnel. 'What I did was tell someone *else* it was worth a hundred bucks. I finessed the truth in order to create a situation.'

'*Finessed the truth*? Well ain't that a lot of fancy wrapping for a plain and simple lie.'

Solomon shook his head. 'Lies are rarely plain, and never simple. Which way?'

'Right. Keep right the whole way down.'

Solomon ducked through another low arch and carried on moving. 'The lie I told about the quarter wasn't even meant for you. And the intended target of a lie is easily as important as the lie itself.'

'Still ended up costing me a steak dinner.'

'Which is why I came back. To try and repay you in some way. Give you something of genuine value.'

Solomon stepped through another entrance to a much larger cave and saw markings covering the far wall. He stopped in front of them and watched the bright torchlight sweep across the petroglyphs as Rita and Asha joined him in the chamber. The symbols were far more vivid than the photograph had shown, the pigments of crushed plants and burnt earth used to decorate the carvings still as bright as when the artist first made them, perfectly preserved in the subterranean blackness away from the bleaching sun.

He traced the outline of the symbols with a pale finger, imagining the Suma artist, working by the light of a flickering flame, chiselling this agreement into water-worn rock so it would be remembered long after his hand had turned to dust, little realizing that one day it might be all that endured of his people. Or not quite. For two still remained on this land, their blood diluted by colonizing tribes so that green Irish eyes now burned in their sun-reddened faces. And what was written here would influence their future, one way or another.

Solomon's eyes traced the symbols, flowing from those he had already seen in the diner photograph to the ones that had been missing. He read the message again, his mind translating the meaning of the petroglyphs until he was certain of what they said. He took a deep breath ready to speak and caught a hint of something in the trapped air of the caves, a faint smell he had not noticed before. He turned his head to one side and listened past the amplified breathing of Rita and her daughter to the sounds beyond.

'What's it say?' Rita said, her whispered voice still loud in the confines of the cave.

Solomon listened a moment longer, breathed in again to confirm the identity of the odour he had caught, then stood back and drew a square with his hands to frame a portion of the wall.

'This is the section shown in the photograph recording an agreement between the chief of these lands, Three Arrows in the Wind, and this man,' he pointed to the symbol of a cow's skull.

'DeVaca,' Rita whispered.

'Álvar Núñez Cabeza deVaca,' Solomon repeated, his voice loud. 'And this is the section not shown in the photograph, the part that identifies deVaca's chief.' He pointed at a symbol of a man on a horse holding a sword in one hand and an arrow in the other. 'The fact that he's on horseback and is carrying an arrow means he *is* a chief, and the addition of the sword means he's foreign, because Native American warriors did not carry swords.'

'The King of Spain?' Asha murmured.

'Possibly.' Solomon moved along the wall. 'Could you shine your light here, please.'

Rita stepped closer and shone the beam on the final few symbols as Solomon ran his hand over them.

'The King of the Spanish Empire at the time of deVaca's expedition was Carlos the fifth, so if this spells that name then we're in business. Unfortunately the Spanish colonials don't have the best of records when it comes to straight dealing. They often made agreements that looked genuine enough but signed it with the wrong name so that it could be ignored later. The way this agreement is written is certainly all proper and correct and it also shows deference. DeVaca is conceding that he and his representatives do not own this land nor do they seek to take it, which is important. It means it was not a spoil of war and liable to be forfeit to whichever nation subsequently laid claim to it through conflict. And because we know from historical records that deVaca was passing through here in the early sixteenth century we also know this agreement pre-dates any subsequent land claims. But to qualify as a legally robust document of title we need the name of deVaca's chief to be recorded and to be correct.' Solomon read the symbols again, making sure he had interpreted them correctly.

Rita took a step forward. 'So what's it say?'

Solomon looked up at her. 'Before I answer, I need to ask you something, and you need to answer me honestly, OK?' Rita nodded. 'Do you really have a gun in your pocket?'

Rita hesitated for a moment then shook her head.

Solomon smiled. 'I didn't think so.' He stood and brushed the dust from his hands. 'Carlos,' he said. 'The last part of the message spells Carlos. DeVaca gave the true name of his king, which means the agreement is genuine and you can legally prove ancestral ownership. If I were you I'd cancel tomorrow's auction and re-list it once it's all been officially proven. This land is worth way more than its current listing.'

Rita stared at Solomon then down at the petroglyphs. 'You sure?'

'Positive. You'll need to get someone from the University of Colorado to ratify it but they'll only tell you what I already did. Congratulations. Your land just quadrupled in value.'

Something shifted in the shadows by the entrance and a torch flicked on, throwing their shadows across the writing on the wall. Rita swung round, the arc of her own torch sweeping across the symbols before settling on the figure who had stepped into the chamber.

It was Daryl Meeks. Flashlight in one hand. Shotgun in the other.

14

'Now ain't this a cosy little scene,' Daryl said. The barrel of the shotgun was pointing in their direction but angled to the ground. 'Y'all want to raise your hands and step a little closer together.'

Rita reached for Asha and instinctively pushed her behind her legs. 'What are you doing, Daryl?'

'Oh, just a bit of due diligence, dotting the "i"s of a potential investment.' His eyes slid over to Solomon. 'I thought I saw you leave.'

'I came back.'

Daryl nodded and the end of the shotgun moved in time. 'Shoulda stayed gone. Better for you. Better for everyone.'

'Now put the gun down, Daryl,' Rita said, 'you're making me nervous.'

'Oh really? I'm sorry.' He smiled but the shotgun stayed where it was.

Rita held her palms out in front of her, like they might protect her from a shotgun blast. 'Put. The damn. Gun down, Daryl.'

Meeks continued to smile. 'Here's the thing about negotiations. If you find yourself in a weak position you don't get to dictate the terms. Now back in the diner there you had a strong position, you had something I wanted and I made you a good offer for it. You turned it down so I had to figure out a way of strengthening my position.' His smile spread. 'And here we are.'

'What was the offer?' Solomon asked.

'Don't matter what the offer was,' Meeks said, 'that offer's gone.'

'What was the offer?' Solomon repeated.

'Are you retarded, boy?' Meeks took a half step forward and shifted the shotgun so it pointed at Solomon. 'I said that offer was dead and if you don't watch your mouth you might be joining it.'

'You're not going to shoot,' Solomon said, still looking at Rita. 'What was the offer and when was it made?'

Rita looked between Meeks and Solomon, fear making her eyes white and wide. 'Sixty thousand,' she said. 'He came to the diner a few hours back with a case full of money.'

'Was anyone else there?'

Rita frowned as she tried to remember. 'Some of the regulars.'

Solomon nodded and looked back at Meeks. 'Then you're not going to shoot.'

'The fuck you say. I've a mind to shoot you right now just to prove you wrong.'

'OK, then shoot. Of course if you do then the sound of the gunshots will be the last thing you ever hear.'

Meeks moved the shotgun up until it was pointing directly at Solomon's face. 'You threatening me, boy?'

'No, merely stating a fact. The shotgun you're holding is a Remington 870, 12 gauge with a discharge noise level of over a hundred and fifty decibels. If you pull the trigger in this enclosed space you'll probably blow out both your eardrums, and that's if you only shoot once. But one shot won't kill us all and you can't afford to leave any witnesses, so you'll have to shoot again, twice probably, to make sure the job's done. Three shotgun blasts from a Remington 870 in this tiny space is going to leave you deaf for life. But that's only the first reason you won't shoot. The second is that three blasts from that gun is going to make all kinds of mess – blood, bone fragments, brains – all over these well-scrutinized and photographed walls. Of course if you manage to buy the land at the auction you could close the caves to the public so no one can ever see what happened here. Only you can't do that, can you? Because you need these lands to be officially recognized as ancestral Indian territory so you can build a casino on it, which means you'll need experts to come here and confirm that these symbols say what you overheard me saying before you stepped into view with that gun in your hand. Now you could try and clean all the mess up but this stone is soft and porous, so not only could stray pellets and bone fragments tear it up, maybe even destroy the petroglyphs entirely, it will also be impossible to remove all the blood evidence from it.

'The third reason you won't shoot is that I told Earl, that truck driver you saw me leaving with, that I was coming back to check on these caves. And he saw your nice, shiny, electric truck with those personalized plates following us out of the diner parking lot and noted your unhealthy interest in me. I told him I'd call him in the morning and tell him what the rest of these symbols said, so if I don't he might get to wondering why not, and when he finds out it was you bought the land and that Rita has disappeared too and you were seen talking to her in the diner, he might start putting it all together and call the local police to tell them what he knows. He might not of course, but it's a risk, and he doesn't trust you much. So there's that.

'But the fourth reason you won't shoot is the biggest of them all, because the fourth reason is you, Daryl Meeks, because whatever image you're trying to project here with your shotgun swagger, you are not a natural killer. Killers don't talk about shooting people, they just go ahead and do it, and yet here we are – talking. You're a talker, a deal maker, not a killer – so why don't we cut all the window dressing and make a deal.'

Meeks stared at Solomon for a moment with an expression that shifted between confusion and surprise, then a large grin spread across his face.

'Man, you sure are cool for a guy with a gun in his face. All right, I'll play along, what kind of deal you got in mind?'

Solomon turned to Rita. 'Name a price.'

Rita blinked and shifted her gaze between Solomon to Meeks. 'I don't . . . I'm not sure . . .'

'It's OK,' Solomon said, drawing her full attention with his eyes, 'I know this is an odd situation but in order for us all to negotiate it safely I need you to try and focus on what you really want to happen. Forget about the petroglyphs and the potential value of this land, just think about what's important to you, right now. What do you want to get out of this?'

'I . . . I want Asha to be safe.'

'Of course, but what else? Think about your future. Think about Asha's future. Say, for argument's sake, you could walk away from here tonight and keep your property, with everything you now know about it, and start the process of getting it recognized as ancestral land, how much money do you think you'd need up front to make all that happen? How long do you think it will take?'

Rita shook her head. 'I don't know.'

'Years,' Solomon said. 'It will take years of your life and hundreds of thousands of dollars you haven't got. I saw your car parked outside the diner earlier, all packed and ready to roll. You're already gone from this place in your head; you just need a little money to set you up wherever you end up, correct?' Rita

73

nodded. 'So what's your price? You must have thought about it. How much do you want right now, tonight, to walk away from this place and never look back? How much do you think you'll need?'

Rita looked across at Meeks. 'I figured . . . a hundred thousand maybe.'

'A hundred grand!' Meeks spat on the ground and shook his head. 'That ain't gonna happen.'

Solomon turned to Meeks, fixing him with his dark eyes. 'I would say that was a reasonable figure.'

'Well you ain't the one being asked to pay it.'

'In the grander scheme of things a hundred thousand dollars is nothing. It buys Rita a fresh start and you get the land you want with no strings, no killing required and no dark cloud hanging over it. You also get the added bonus of keeping your hearing – what price can you put on that?'

Meeks smiled and shook his head. 'You think you're real smart, don't you?' He began to lower himself down but kept his eyes on Solomon. 'You think you got this situation all figured out, telling me all the reasons why I ain't gonna shoot you.' He placed his flashlight on the ground so it was still pointing at them then stood up again and reached behind his back with his free hand. 'Thing is, Mr Smart Guy, you don't know everything. And this shotgun here ain't the only gun I brung to the party.'

His hand reappeared holding a pistol. 'Now this here's a Glock-9 automatic. Much more precise weapon, lot quieter too. If I shoot you with this it won't make nearly so much mess, but you'll be just as dead. Now what do you think about that?'

Solomon studied the gun for a moment then looked back up at Meeks. 'I think that only solves one of your four problems. But, fine, if you genuinely fancy your chances as they stand, go ahead. Shoot.'

Meeks pointed the pistol at Solomon's face and shuffled his feet like he was sighting in on a target in a shooting range.

Solomon saw the skin on Meeks's finger go white as it tightened on the trigger. He was aware of Rita pushing Asha further behind her. He turned his head to her. 'Do you have a will?'

'What?' Her eyes were white and wide and fixed on the gun.

'A will. Do you have one?'

Rita blinked as she tried to process the question. 'No.'

Solomon turned back to Meeks. 'That's the fifth reason you're not going to shoot us.'

Meeks frowned. 'What's Rita's will got to do with anything?'

'If you shoot us then Rita won't be around tomorrow to sign over legal ownership of the land so they'll have to postpone any sale until she does show up, which she won't. So the land will be trapped in legal limbo until she can officially be declared dead, which in the state of Texas takes seven years. Then, with no will in place, they'll have to do their due diligence and look for any next of kin, which will take at least another year, by which time the University of Colorado will have had ample time to go through their archives, find the photographs they took of this cave the last time they were here and let the whole world know what it says. So, when the state eventually takes ownership they might not even sell it, they might just develop it themselves, or if they do put it to auction there'll be a bidding war that will push the price up so high you will look back at the time you could have bought it for a hundred thousand dollars as the best deal you ever let slide.'

Solomon paused to let the truth of what he was saying register. 'Or, you can give Rita a hundred thousand dollars right now, she signs over the deeds, no one is any the wiser about what took place here and we all go our separate ways.'

Meeks adjusted his grip on the Glock. 'What's in it for you?'

Solomon smiled. 'I get to not die in this cave.'

Meeks looked across at Rita then back at Solomon. 'How do I know you won't go running to the police the moment I set you loose?'

'And tell them what? That you held us at gunpoint and forced us to take a hundred thousand dollars? I bet you're quite the public figure around here, aren't you? A man of means and influence. A provider of jobs. Who's going to believe the word of a stranger and a diner waitress over someone like that?'

Meeks's eyes dropped down to where Asha was peering out from behind Rita's legs then looked away again. 'I don't have a hundred grand,' he said. 'Not that I can lay my hands on tonight.'

Solomon smiled and dropped his hands down to his side. 'How much *can* you get?'

76

15

Rita drove. Solomon sat next to her, his usual nausea from being inside a moving car making him wish they would hurry up and get to wherever it was they were going. They were in Meeks's silver pick-up, its electric engine whining in the night like some great mosquito on the hunt for blood.

'Take the next right,' Meeks said. Solomon could feel the pressure of the Glock sticking into the back of his seat and the barrel of the shotgun moved in and out of his peripheral vision along with the movement of the car, pointing vaguely at Rita. Asha was in the back with Meeks, her eyes wide and shining in the dark. She hadn't said a single word since Meeks had stepped into the cave. She was in shock most likely, another reason Solomon wanted to get this done quickly.

'Are the guns still necessary?' he asked.

Meeks snorted. 'So says the man who ain't got none. I'll put away the firepower soon as the deal's done. Now take that right.'

Rita made the turn onto a graded track that made the shotgun barrel bump around a little more and headed away from the main road towards a faint glow of light ahead. It grew steadily brighter until it took the form of a large house built like an old, adobe-style hacienda. It was surrounded by empty horse corrals, like it was trying to look like a ranch without actually being one. There was a large, covered garage area over to one side with a selection of shiny vehicles parked beneath it: two Harleys, a Range Rover, an Audi Spyder, and a fully tricked-out Ford F150 pick-up with blacked-out glass and extra-large wheels.

'Not a particularly eco-friendly fleet,' Solomon observed as his head filled with information and technical specifications.

Daryl smiled and seemed to puff up a little. 'Every boy gotta have his toys. I drive this electric number for show mostly. Wouldn't sell many renewables if I went to every meeting in a gas guzzler. Them there's my private passions. You can't beat the sound of a V8 to get the heart pumping.'

The silver pick-up slid to a silent halt in front of the main entrance and Daryl got out, slipping the Glock into his waistband but keeping his shotgun pointed inside the car.

'Come on out,' he said, 'nice and slow. This Remington's got a hair trigger so don't be doing nuthin' stupid.'

Solomon got out first and stepped away from the car to draw Meeks's aim. Rita got out of the driver's side and opened the door for Asha who immediately clung to her mother's legs.

'Toss me the keys over, nice and slow,' Meeks said.

Rita threw them underarm and he caught them one-handed then backed up to the front door, unlocked it and deactivated the alarm with an electronic button on the key ring.

He nodded at the open door. 'You first. I'll tell you where to go. Stay nice and tight and don't even think about trying anything,' he held up the button. 'This here's a panic button for the alarm. If I press it the cops'll be down on this house in less than five minutes. Now you might be thinking "*Great! Bring it on.*" Only you should know I go drinking with most of those fellas, so they ain't gonna believe a damn word you tell 'em, and you ain't gonna tell 'em a thing 'cause all they're gonna find here is some intruders I shot dead while defending my property.'

He looked at Asha and smiled. 'I won't shoot you though. Not even my cop buddies are gonna believe a little kid like you was creepin' around at night fixin' to rob me. But I do know some folks'll take care of you for me.' He looked up at Rita. 'You would not believe some of the people I do business with, specially on the Mexican side of the border. Pretty little thing like her should fetch me an even prettier price.' He let the meaning sink in for a moment then flashed her a broad smile. 'But if y'all just play nice and do exactly what I say then none of that's gonna happen, we can all stay friends and be on our separate ways before morning.'

Solomon could feel Rita vibrating next to him, the anger within her like a contained explosion. Daryl was close enough that he could take the shotgun from him if he wanted. Grab the barrel and angle it up so it would discharge in the air when he pulled the trigger then twist it out of his grip and have it pointing back at him before he knew what had happened. But then what would he do? Shoot him? Call the local cops, who also happened to be Meeks's drinking buddies?

No.

He had another idea, one that would work out better for everyone, or almost everyone. All he had to do was keep things moving in the right direction.

He turned to Rita and whispered, 'It's just talk. None of what he said will happen because we're going to do what he wants, right?'

Rita looked at him and he could see fire burning behind her green eyes.

'Right!?' he repeated, holding her gaze and forcing her to focus on him instead of Meeks.

Her eyes continued to blaze for a second before she blinked, like a spell had been broken, then moved towards the house, pushing Asha ahead to keep her as far away from Meeks as possible. Solomon followed and passed through the front door into a large, double-height hallway with twin, curving staircases rising up either side of a mechanical bull.

'Another of my little toys,' Daryl explained. 'Sometimes I get the fellas round for an evening and we drink tequila and ride that bitch all night long. Go straight on past on the right and head down the first set of stairs you come across.'

They moved forward, their footsteps echoing in the vast hallway. The decor was a weird mix of mock classical and frontier brutalism, all white marble and heavy wooden furniture as if a Roman senator had hung up his toga and decided to become a Texas rancher. It felt unlived-in and sterile in a way that made the house seem both full and empty at the same time. Large pictures decorated white walls, big, garish oil paintings of rodeo riders and desert sunsets in heavy gold frames, like a kid's idea of what a grown-up might hang in a house. There were a couple of portraits of Meeks too. In one he was astride a rearing stallion; the other had him strad-dling a Harley and staring into the middle distance.

They reached the staircase and headed down it. Asha first, Rita and Solomon next, Meeks bringing up the rear, shotgun in hand and pointing down at them. The air cooled as they dropped into the bedrock beneath the house. Another portrait greeted them at the bottom of the stairs showing a thin, stern-looking man in monochrome work clothes. He stared out at the world above their heads while a geyser of oil blew out from a drilling tower behind him. The artist who'd painted it possessed more talent than whoever had done the ones of Meeks and the likeness was clear. Dear old dad. Standing in front of the stroke of pure, dumb luck that had made this house and everything in it possible.

'Stop there,' Meeks said, and moved past them to a door at the end of the hallway. There was an electronic keypad set into it and he masked it with his body as he entered the code, like a nervous old lady at a cashpoint. A deep clunking sound echoed down the hallway then Meeks leaned against the door and it swung open slowly. 'Welcome to my inner sanctum,' he said, stepping into the room and causing lights to blink on from some hidden sensor. 'Come on in. Nice and slow.'

They followed him inside, Solomon taking the lead now, and he noted the thickness of the doorframe as he passed through it. The room beyond was a vault made to look like a study. A large desk dominated the space with a fancy leather chair behind it and various cabinets lining the walls. Some held files but most displayed guns – rifles, shotguns, handguns – all carefully lit so their pearl handles and metal blue surfaces shone like beetles in a museum exhibit. Meeks moved past the desk, ran his hand down the side of a rifle cabinet and it slid aside to reveal a safe in the wall behind it. He stared into a small peephole set into the door and another deep thunk sounded then the door sprang open.

'Retina recognition,' Meeks said, like he was trying to sell it to them. 'State of the art. More accurate than a fingerprint.'

There were only two items in the safe, a leather briefcase and a wooden box. He took both out and carried them over to the desk.

He opened the wooden box first and lifted out an antique-looking revolver from its cushion of velvet.

'This here was my daddy's gun and his daddy's afore his,' he said, holding it up to the light and turning it in his hand. 'My granddaddy told me one time how he'd shot a man dead with it. Said he was a scout for an oil outfit who'd heard about the tar sands we had on our land and came poking around where he

81

wasn't invited. Granddaddy told him to get lost but found him snooping around the next day, trespassing on our land, so he dealt him out a little Texas justice.'

He spun the cylinder and looked at Solomon until it stopped clicking. 'That is to say we take property pretty seriously down here.' He reached into his jacket, pulled out an envelope and pushed it across the desk towards Rita. 'That's why I need you to sign this letter I showed you earlier. To make everything all legal and proper.'

Rita stared at the envelope then flicked her eyes up to the antique revolver. 'Texas justice,' she said. 'Is that where your people get to steal my people's land at gunpoint?'

Meeks smiled. 'I ain't stealing nothing, sweetheart. I'm giving you a fair price, more'n fair, and everyone has their price.' He opened the briefcase. 'Way I see it, I came to see you earlier and made you an offer. You turned it down and I have a witness to that. Several in fact, and one who is a legal representative of the court.'

'Your lawyer,' Rita said. 'He ain't exactly impartial.'

'You're missing the point. What I'm saying is I have witnesses that will say I made you a fair, pre-emptive offer. Now I could make you take that offer, I am holding a gun on you after all. But to sweeten the deal and ensure there are no hard feelings going forward I'm going to give you all the money in this case, all the cash I can put my hand to right now.' He pushed it across the table towards her. 'Almost eighty thousand dollars. Now please understand that, not only am I doing you a favour here by upping my offer when I don't really have to, I'm also buying your silence. You take this money and you leave. I don't ever want to see you or your kid around here again, you hear?'

'And what's in it for me?' Solomon asked.

'What's in it for you?' Meeks laughed and shook his head.

82

'What's in it for you is that I don't put a bullet in your face then go bury you out in the desert like they did with her baby daddy.'

Rita tensed. 'What's that you say?'

Meeks stared at her like he wasn't sure what she meant. Then he whooped and slapped his leg and shook his head, laughing.

'You didn't know? Well shit, you people don't know nuthin', do ya. I thought everybody knew what happened to . . . what was his name now?'

'Eddie,' Rita said. 'His name was Eddie.'

'That's right, Eddie. Fact I'm pretty sure everybody *does* know. I guess no one bothered to tell you.' He turned to Solomon like he was telling the story to a buddy at a bar. 'So anyway ole Eddie gets this idea to try and put together a decent score to help her fix up the diner and, damn fool that he was, ends up borrowing a roll off some bad dudes out of El Paso. Only the money he borrowed ain't quite enough to do all the things he wants to get done. Way I heard it he wanted to marry her, buy her a ring and pay for a fancy wedding, the whole bit. So he goes over to the Lucky Res and tries to gamble it up a little. Loses it all and a whole lot more. So now he's in the hole to the casino *and* the dudes in El Paso and he cain't pay neither one of 'em. I don't know who caught up with him first. Don't really matter, the end result was always going to be the same.' He made a gun with his hand and put it to the side of his head. 'Boom. The coyotes will have ate 'im and scattered his bones long since if they didn't bury him deep enough.' He shrugged. 'Texas justice.'

Rita looked down at Asha who was staring at nothing, her eyes wide and glazed with shock.

'Give me the damn pen,' she said. 'I'll sell you the land. I don't want any part of it any more. There's too much blood in it. Too much blood and too many people who don't give a damn about doing the right thing by nobody.'

Meeks handed her his pen. 'Don't be too sore. They was probably just trying to spare your feelings.'

Rita grabbed the pen and uncapped it. She ripped open the envelope and smoothed the paperwork down ready to sign. She didn't realize she was no longer holding the pen until Solomon held it up and pointed it down at the empty case.

'How much is in there?' he said. 'I mean exactly.'

Meeks regarded him with a look somewhere between surprise and caution. Solomon had moved so fast to pluck the pen from Rita's hand that he was figuring out if he might be able to grab his gun as fast and was glad the desk was between them.

'What the hell business is it of yours?' he said.

'Well you're pointing a gun at me and you want me to keep my mouth shut, and if you tell me how much is in the case I will.'

Meeks frowned then shook his head and smiled to ease the growing tension in the room. 'What the hell,' he said. 'There's seventy-eight thousand, nine hundred and twenty dollars there. Happy now?'

Solomon shook his head slowly, like it confirmed some privately held suspicion. 'Not enough,' he said.

Meeks raised his gun a little higher and cocked his head to one side like he hadn't heard properly. 'What's that?'

'I said it's not enough. You're eighty dollars short.'

Meeks laughed. 'Eighty dollars! There's almost eighty grand in that case and you're bitching about a few more bucks.'

Solomon shrugged. 'Everyone has their price, you said so yourself. Mine is eighty dollars.'

'But I done told you already, that there cash is all I can put my hand to right now, so I ain't got no eighty dollars. And I sure as hell ain't waiting around here all night swapping stories and waiting for the banks to open, so you're just going to have to take it or leave it.'

'It's OK,' Rita said, holding her hand out for the pen. 'I'll sign the damn papers.'

'What about your wallet?' Solomon said, his eyes still fixed on Meeks.

'My what?'

'You have a wallet in your back pocket, I can see the outline of it. How much you got in that?'

Meeks stared at Solomon down the barrel of his granddaddy's pistol and everything seemed to pause for a long, long moment until he blew out a long stream of air and lowered the gun.

'Goddammit you are a pain in the ass, my friend. Lucky for you I'm not the kind of guy to shoot someone over a few lousy bucks.' He reached into his back pocket, pulled out a thick, leather wallet with 'DM' stitched into it and tossed it onto the desk. 'Pick my pocket, why don't you.'

Solomon picked up the wallet and flipped it open. There was a thick stack of credit cards inside as well as a few bills. He pulled them out: three twenties, a ten, a five and six ones. Eighty-one dollars.

'It's a dollar too much,' Solomon said.

'Keep the change,' Meeks sneered. 'Now give her the pen and sign the damned paperwork before I lose my patience and shoot the damn lot of you.'

16

Rita signed.

Meeks checked everything was all dotted and crossed correctly then smiled and locked the papers in his safe along with his granddaddy's pistol.

'Out in the hall with you,' he said, the shotgun still slung under his arm, 'over by my daddy's portrait where I can see you.' Then he locked the study door with the shotgun inside and held up his hands to show they were empty. 'All friends now,' he said. 'And to prove there's no hard feelings I'm going to give y'all a ride home.'

The Glock was still tucked into his waistband but Solomon chose not to mention it. Meeks wasn't going to use it now. He thought he'd won.

Meeks led them outside, made them hop into the flat bed of the Ford pick-up then drove them back to the diner, like a team boss taking melon-picking migrants out to the fields. Rita hugged Asha the whole way, stroking her hair. No one said anything.

They pulled up outside the diner and Meeks stayed in the truck, engine running, until they'd climbed down.

'Have a nice life, y'all,' he shouted out the window as he pulled away. 'And if I ever see any one of you round here again you won't find me so friendly.'

Then he floored the gas and sent arcs of dirt into the air as he fishtailed back to the blacktop then away up the road. Rita gathered Asha into her arms, hugging her hard and squinting against the cloud of grit until the red tail-lights and deep roar of the engine melted away in the night.

'Asshole,' she said, then she kissed Asha, held her face in her hands and looked her in the eyes. 'Go fetch anything you need from inside 'cause this is the last chance you'll get, OK? We're heading out in five. And fetch some water and something to snack on in the car, we're going to be on the road for a long while.'

Asha nodded then headed off in a daze, the bell tinkling above the door as she stepped inside. Rita waited until the door banged shut again then turned on Solomon.

'What the hell were you playing at back there, asking for eighty dollars when he had a goddam gun pointing at my baby? Eighty dollars! Are you crazy? You took an unnecessary risk that put me and my daughter in danger and for what? For eighty lousy bucks!'

'He was never going to shoot,' Solomon said.

'You do not know that. You might think you know everything but you don't. Daryl Meeks is a mean, spiteful, spoiled little brat who's done whatever he wanted his entire life and thinks he can get away with anything on account of the fact he probably already has. You don't know him. You don't. Why did you even do it, it wasn't even your money?'

'You said you needed a hundred thousand dollars to start a new life. I was just trying to get you a little closer.'

'By eighty bucks! What the hell difference is that going to make? Eighty dollars makes no difference to me whatsoever, but being alive sure does.'

87

Solomon cocked his head to one side and seemed to study her anger like it was some kind of exotic creature that had flown out of the night.

'You'll see,' he said. 'When you get to wherever you're going you'll realize that eighty dollars makes all the difference in the world.'

'No, I won't,' Rita said. 'One motel room, a few burgers and a tank of gas and that eighty dollars will be gone but I'll still be pissed at you. I'll be pissed at you and what happened here tonight forever, you and Meeks both. I wish you'd never come here. I wish you'd never stepped through that door and spun your lies or told me what was written on the cave walls. Because even though I probably got more for the land than I might, I wish I'd not learned what I learned tonight. I'd rather stayed ignorant and poorer.'

'Being unaware of the truth does not change what that truth is.'

'Oh shut up. Just shut your damn mouth. Don't talk to me any more or I might end up punching you square in the face. My daughter's coming back and she's already been through enough for one night.'

'You'll understand,' Solomon said. 'When you get to where you're going you'll understand.'

The bell above the door tinkled again and Asha reappeared juggling her school bag, some bottles of water and a large bag of nachos.

'Let me help,' Solomon said, stepping forward and plucking the bag from her shoulder just as it was about to slide off. He took it to the back of the car, opened the tailgate and managed to squeeze it into a small space amongst the tight jumble of possessions inside.

'Thanks,' Rita said, slamming the tailgate shut. 'Get in the car, Ash, we're leaving.'

Asha looked over at Solomon, smiled at him then walked round to the passenger side and got in.

'There's an old Suma legend about this land,' Solomon said. 'It holds that so long as the blood of Three Arrows in the Wind remains upon this land then the sun will rise and the sun will set and the rivers will flow to the sea.'

Rita nodded. 'Uh huh? So what happens when we leave, the sun not going to rise tomorrow morning? Daryl Meeks is going to be awful pissed off when he finds out he done bought a piece of dark desert.'

Solomon smiled. 'The legend also says that whoever takes this land will know nothing but tears.'

'Really?' Rita shook her head. 'That's just not how it works. People like Daryl Meeks always win in the end, and people like me get to pour their drinks and mop up their mess.' She looked over at the diner one last time. 'Least I won't be cleaning up after anyone else for a while.'

She opened the driver's door. 'I'd offer you a lift but we ain't got room and I'm too mad at you.' She nodded down the road past the neon sign saying '*BOBBY D's EATS*'. 'Most of the traffic heads east. Keep your thumb out and you'll catch a ride sooner or later.'

Then she got in the car, turned on the engine and drove away.

17

Daryl Meeks struggled to sleep, the thrill of the night's events and thoughts of the river of money that would flow his way buzzing in his restless mind. A friend of his once told him the Lucky Reservation Casino averaged three million dollars profit a *week*. Three *million* dollars. That was way more money than they'd ever made from oil, even when all the wells had been producing, and unlike oil money this was a river of cash that would never run dry.

He lay in bed, adding up figures in his head – three million a week, twelve million a month, one hundred and forty-four million a year – until the numbers got too big and he gave up on sleep entirely, threw off the covers and marched down to the basement where the portrait of his daddy hung. He looked up at it for a long time and with all kinds of emotions roiling inside him – pride, resentment, elation, anger. His daddy had never thought very highly of him, never thought he would amount to anything more than a kind of shadow of himself, elevated solely by the family name and the money he'd made and put in his pocket. A lot of other people round here thought the same.

Well let's just see what they got to say when I build me a casino on that patch of old Indian land no one else thought was worth a damn.

He stared up at his daddy's portrait, wishing he was still alive so he could see what his son had done, and how much money he'd make, so much that it would make all those oil dollars seem like loose change. But the expression on his daddy's face remained unchanged, his nose raised high like the whole world was beneath him.

'*Fuck you, old man,*' Daryl said at last, then headed to the kitchen to make himself some coffee.

He'd waited for the sun to rise then driven over to Nate Prime's place to tell him the news and give him the signed paperwork to file. Then he'd driven out to the diner, parked out back and walked out to the caves and taken detailed photographs of every inch of the decorated walls so he could email them over to the University of Colorado and start the ball rolling on getting it all authenticated. Then he'd hiked back and stepped through the door of the diner.

His diner.

He stood there for a moment, watching dust drifting through the slanted morning light, listening to the stillness and the occasional sound of a vehicle passing out on the highway. He felt calm. In control. Powerful.

He looked around to see what Rita had taken but as far as he could tell she hadn't taken a damn thing. Even the dusty old Indian souvenirs were still there beneath the faded photograph of the symbols on the cave wall. He walked across the cracked vinyl floor, took one of the souvenir caps with '*A gift from Broken Promise, Texas*' embroidered on it then bashed the dust off it and fitted it on his head. He glanced up at the painted menu from beneath the brim and a low hunger shifted inside him. He hadn't eaten anything since lunch the previous day when that smart-ass stranger had walked in here with his wager and his weird ways.

Not so smart now, are you, mister?

He passed through the gap in the counter and into the kitchen. There was nothing here worth salvaging or selling either, everything was old and battered and oil-stained. He opened the fridge, found some frozen slices of ham and a few eggs and fiddled around with the hot plate until he got it working then threw some ham slices on to defrost while it heated up. Next he checked the cupboards and found a half-empty catering pack of coffee and an open box of filters. He set a fresh pot gurgling and paced back and forth behind the counter while his head buzzed with all the things he needed to do.

First thing was to start the process of authenticating the land as ancestral Indian property. Then he needed to get on to the state gaming board and get that ball rolling too. He also needed to hire architects and engineers to start designing everything and putting all the permits in place, all of which would require seed cash and proper financing. He could use his own money to get things started but he didn't have the kind of cash to build a casino. Besides, it wasn't just the finance he needed. He'd also want people with heavyweight political muscle and influence in city hall in his corner, because none of this was going to be a cake walk. The tribal elders at the Lucky Res up the road would try and block the development the whole way; they didn't want a rival operation springing up in the next county to take a big bite out of their pie.

Three million dollars a week.

That was what he needed to focus on. Keep his eye on the prize and the ball rolling. Two years from now, three tops, he'd be standing here leaning against one of those glass bars lit from the inside, sipping on a cocktail and watching a river of money flow past on its way to his bank account.

The sudden sound made Daryl jump. It had come from the

old payphone by the counter, a loud, metallic *dringgg* designed to cut through the noise in busy public places. It rang again, sharp and loud, and it occurred to him that it might be Nate Prime trying to get a hold of him for some reason because the cellphone reception here was shit, something else he needed to fix. He grabbed the phone midway through its next ring and lifted it to his ear.

'Bobby D's,' he said, like he'd heard Rita do a million times before when truckers called ahead to make their orders.

'Hi, I'm looking for a Rita Treepoint.' It was a woman's voice.

'She's not here.'

'Do you know how I might get hold of her?'

Daryl shrugged. 'Her cell maybe.'

'I tried that already but got voicemail. She left a message last night and asked me to get back to her urgently. Said she wanted to speak to me ahead of the sale of some land in a place called Broken Promise, Texas.'

'Who is this, please?'

'My name is Doctor Andrea Thompson. I'm calling from the Center for Native American and Indigenous Studies at the University of Colorado.'

Daryl's face broke into a smile. 'Yes. That's . . . I left you a message too. Name's Meeks. Daryl Meeks. I called about the same thing – the cave symbols – but you can call the dogs off, ain't no need to talk to Rita no more. She would have been calling to find out what those symbols said before she sold the land but I done bought it already.'

'Oh. I was under the impression she wanted to speak to me before any sale went ahead.'

'Well no. See, you're talking to the new owner now, so any information you have regarding it you can tell to me, though I already know what you're going to say.'

93

'Really?'

'Yes, ma'am.'

'How? Can you read Western Suma?'

Daryl smiled. 'No, ma'am, but I know a man who can.'

There was a slight pause. 'But the only people who can read Western Suma are on my team, and they're all women.'

Daryl felt the skin tighten on his neck. 'Yes but. There was this fella came through here yesterday. He was . . . he knew all kinds of stuff . . . I can tell you what he said.'

He grabbed the photograph from the wall. 'The cow's head,' he said, grasping at a memory. 'That stands for deVaca.'

'That's right. Álvar Núñez Cabeza deVaca.'

'There you go,' Daryl felt his confidence returning. 'And the figure on horseback, the one with three arrows over it. That means *Three Arrows in the Wind*. He was chief of this area way back in the fifteen hundreds or sixteen hundreds or whenever.'

'Sixteen hundreds,' Doctor Thompson said. 'DeVaca passed through West Texas in 1534.'

'Bingo. And Three Arrows in the Wind was Rita's . . . er, I mean Ms Treepoint's ancestor. Three arrows, Treepoint – you see? The symbols are kind of an agreement between the chief of these lands and this deVaca fella.'

'Well yes, that's exactly right. But how do you . . .?'

'Like I said, this guy swept through yesterday who could read it.'

'Did he tell you about the signature?'

'He told us all of it. He said the signature had to be of a historically recognized figure in order to make it legal and that the King of Spain at the time of this deVaca character was Charles the somethingth.'

'Carlos the fifth.'

'There you go.' Daryl fumbled his cellphone from his pocket

and opened the photos, looking for a clear shot of the last part of the message. He found one and zoomed in so the signature part filled his screen. 'OK, I got it. There's a bent cross which is a C, right?'

'Yes. Yes, it is.'

Daryl laughed. 'There you go, C for Carlos.'

There was a pause, just long enough for a little crack of doubt to form, then Doctor Thompson drove a wedge into it.

'It doesn't spell Carlos,' she said.

Daryl's smile froze. 'But this guy, he said . . .' He zoomed in on his phone until the image started to pixellate.

'It doesn't spell Carlos,' Doctor Thompson repeated. Daryl heard the rustle of paper again then the tapping of keys. 'When I got Ms Treepoint's message I pulled up the archive photos we have. I'm looking at them now. That symbol next to the bent cross, the circle with the two lines through it, that's a "U" not an "A". Then we have the two hatched lines, which is an "L", and the symbol like an eye is an "O".'

Daryl stared at the photo of the petroglyphs on his phone, his eyes passing over each symbol as Doctor Thompson described it.

'Then what does it say?' he murmured, his brain too jangled to be able to string the letters together or make sense of them.

'It spells CULO,' Doctor Thompson replied. 'It was a common trick of the conquistadors to make deals that appeared genuine but were written in such a way that they were actually meaningless. This is a prime example. Everything is legitimate until the very end when deVaca signs off in a way that not only invalidates the agreement but also pokes fun at the chief he's striking a deal with. He would have known the Indians didn't understand Spanish so he signed it off with an insult. Not Carlos but Culo. Culo is Spanish for "ass".'

The room seemed to shift and the phone fell from Daryl's hand and banged against the wall. He reached out to grab the countertop to stop himself from collapsing. His knees felt weak and he was short of breath. He could hear a tiny voice that sounded like it was coming from a long way off and he realized that Doctor Thompson was still talking. He reached for the phone and brought it back to his ear.

'Hello!' Doctor Thompson said. 'Are you still there?'

'Yes,' Daryl managed.

'You OK?'

'Yes,' he said again, then hung up and collapsed onto a stool, taking deep breaths to try and stop the room from spinning. It couldn't be right. Maybe she'd been looking at the wrong photographs, some other markings on some other cave. Only she hadn't. The symbols she'd described were the same as the ones on the photos he'd taken that morning.

He took more breaths, long and deep, and smelt something sharp and acrid. He rose to his feet and stumbled to the kitchen where the two ham slices he'd thrown on the hot plate to defrost were now smoking and curled up and black at the edges. He spotted a fire extinguisher fixed to the wall by the back door and lunged for it, pulling it free just as the charcoaled edges caught flame and started to burn. He tugged at the safety pin and pointed the extinguisher at the fire. It had already spread across the surface of the hot plate, throwing up curls of black smoke as the oil burned.

The pin came loose and he was about to press the lever to discharge the foam when a thought struck him. Nate Prime had already set up interim insurance on this place, which meant the building was now insured in his name. He couldn't remember the exact amount but it was around thirty thousand dollars, enough to mitigate his losses. A loss adjuster would come and try and screw him but it wasn't that big a claim so he wouldn't bust his balls too much. Besides, who was to say what might have happened here? Maybe Rita forgot to turn something off before she left. Or something switched itself on on a timer and there was no one here to notice. Either way this building was worth more to him as a smoking pile of embers than a diner. And it was Rita's place. So let it burn.

He put the extinguisher back in its holder and wiped it down with his sleeve. Next he wiped all the cupboard handles and surfaces he'd touched, keeping low as he moved past the burning hot plate, away from the smoke and the worst of the heat. Out in the diner he wiped down the coffee pot and the payphone then looked around trying to remember what else he might have touched. He checked the road to see if it was clear then hurried out back to his car and was back on the road before the smoke had started to rise above the roof.

Sooner or later someone would spot that the diner was on fire and call it in, but by then it would be too late. The nearest fire truck was in Van Horn and it would take at least twenty minutes to get here. By then the whole place would be nothing but ashes and flame. He glanced in the rear-view mirror, checking to see if anyone was on the road behind him, and saw that he was still wearing the cap he'd taken. He took it off and threw it on the passenger seat. A souvenir of Broken Promise, Texas. Man had that place ever been named right.

But Daryl had also made a promise that wasn't true and he warmed his hands now at the memory of it. Last night when Rita said she needed a hundred grand to start afresh he'd said he couldn't lay his hands on that much cash. But there was another safe in his office, filled with bearer bonds and gold bars and at least another fifty grand in cash. That uppity motherfucker who thought he knew everything had not known about that now, had he? He could easily have given Rita a hundred grand but he'd kept his head in a tight spot and had only given her seventy-nine thousand. The asshole had been oddly particular about that number for some reason. Daryl figured he must be one of those autistics, like Rain Man or something. That would explain how he knew so much random stuff about random shit. Probably also why he wanted such an exact figure. But in the end he wasn't so smart. He hadn't known about Daryl's other safe and he hadn't known what those damn symbols said in the cave neither. And Rita was off down the road in search of her new life with twenty-one grand less than she coulda had and Daryl felt good about that. He felt good that her old home was burning down too. Then he saw the billboard ahead for the Lucky Reservation Casino and the phrase '*Three million dollars profit a week*' popped back into his head.

He didn't feel so good after that.

18

Rita had driven solidly for the best part of ten hours when tiredness finally overtook her. She'd intended to drive until night fell again and put at least a couple of states between them and the events of the previous night but the long miles and the bright sun and endlessly rolling road had gradually worn her down until even the simple act of keeping her eyes open required an almost superhuman effort.

She looked over at Asha, asleep in the passenger seat. She'd fallen asleep soon after they'd left Broken Promise and Rita had let her stay that way, aware that it was probably the best antidote to the poisonous night she'd had and doubly aware that when she woke up they'd have to talk about it all. It wasn't the humiliation of being forced to sign away her property at the point of a gun that galled her most, or the fact that Asha had been witness to it all; it was the casual discovery that Eddie was dead and everyone in town seemed to know about it, at least that's what Meeks had said. And though she normally didn't believe one word in ten that came out of his mouth, in this particular case she believed him. Why would he lie about it? There was nothing in it for him, and Daryl Meeks never did anything for free. She'd thought the people of Broken Promise were her friends, that everyone there looked out for everyone. Turned out they'd been no better than lying to her the whole time.

'Honey,' she said softly. Asha stirred in the passenger seat but didn't wake. 'Honey,' she repeated, a little louder this time.

Asha stretched and opened her eyes, blinking against the sunshine. She looked outside the window at the passing landscape. Tall fir trees lined the road and flashed past in a smear of green.

'Where are we?'

'Colorado somewhere. Listen, I need to stop. I'm so tired that if I don't lie down soon I'm going to drive us into a ditch.'

Asha rubbed her eyes and peered ahead, her younger eyes spotting a sign further down the road. 'There's a motel or something up ahead.'

Rita eased off the gas a little and focused on the sign like it was the finishing line at the end of a long, long race. It was maybe half a mile further but she was so tired she wasn't even sure she could make it.

'You don't have to worry about me, you know,' Asha said suddenly.

'I'm not . . . why do you . . . what made you say that?'

'Because of what Daryl Meeks said about Dad. I figure you're probably worrying about me, but I kind of knew he was never coming back. I mean it's sad that he got himself killed, but he was trying to get some money together for you, for us, just like he said he was. And that's kinda cool, you know? So I'm sad that he's never coming back, but mostly I'm happy. Happy that he didn't run away from us. That he kept his word but was just unlucky is all. He was a good guy. My dad was a good guy. And that's awesome.'

Rita felt hot, stinging tears rise up and she let them fall. She was too tired to stop them anyway. Her beautiful, earnest, serious daughter had just stuck a pin right through the heart of thoughts that had been whirling around in her head for practically the whole drive.

'Mom?' Asha said, with the questioning tone in her voice she'd had ever since she could talk.

'What, honey?'

'Do you believe in angels?'

'What?'

'I've been thinking about that man who came to the diner and told us what the symbols said.'

'Solomon. His name was Solomon.'

'Solomon,' Asha repeated, like it was a magic word. 'Who was he?'

Rita shrugged. 'I ain't sure but he weren't no angel. He was just some drifter looking for a free meal.'

'But don't you think it was funny, him turning up like that when the land was about to be sold, and being able to read those symbols that nobody else could read, so it made the land worth more? Also, why did he stand up to Daryl Meeks like he did? I mean, he had a gun but that Solomon didn't seem scared at all and it made me not feel scared too. He stood up to Daryl Meeks and told him to his face that he weren't gonna shoot us and I believed him. Why did he do all that, do you think, when he didn't need to and when he didn't get nothing out of it? I think he turned up for a reason. To watch over us maybe.'

'You think he was some kind of a . . . guardian angel?'

'Yeah. Maybe.'

'Honey. He lied to me about some coin he had in order to con me out of a steak dinner, then he put us at risk, and for what? To squeeze a few more measly dollars out of Daryl Meeks. He weren't no angel. He was just another macho asshole making life difficult for us.'

101

'Eighty dollars,' Asha murmured.

'What?'

'Eighty-one dollars actually. He was real particular about that figure and seemed happy when he got it. I wonder why that was?'

Rita rubbed her eyes and forced them to stay open for just a little longer. 'Well I guess we'll never know. Maybe I can figure it out once I've had some sleep.'

She turned off the road past a sign saying '*Pagosa Springs Inn. Free WiFi. Free Breakfast. Free Parking*' then followed the track to a cluster of buildings that looked like miniature log cabins. She pulled into a parking spot by the office and cut the engine. 'Wait here while I check us in.'

She got a key to a double room and drove round to a cabin with a view of the mountains that she had no intention of enjoying until she walked into the room and saw them framed by the big picture window. They were tall and craggy and monumental and fringed by fir-tree forests that looked like they should have snow on their boughs and probably did in winter. It was about as different a vista from anything in Broken Promise as it was possible to get and the sight of it made her relax in a way she hadn't been able to since she'd started driving. Because they weren't in Texas any more and because Asha was OK.

She sank down on the edge of a bed and stared out at the view, dimly aware of Asha, moving around in the background, checking out the bathroom and unpacking stuff from her bag. Maybe they'd stay here, find a house with a view of the mountains. She couldn't imagine ever getting tired of looking at them. She wondered whether seventy-nine thousand dollars would be enough to put a down payment on a nice place and again felt a slight tug of regret that she didn't have just a little bit more.

'Mom?' The questioning tone was back.

'Uh huh?'

'I think I know why Solomon made Daryl give us those eighty-one dollars.'

Rita looked round. Asha was standing by her bed. Her backpack was open, the contents were spread around it. She had something in her hand, a small piece of paper that she held out for Rita to take.

It was a thin slip of paper with the logo of the Lucky Reservation Casino embossed on the top and an amount made out to cash and printed in figures and words. Twenty-one thousand dollars.

It took a moment for her sleep-starved brain to figure out what it was and what it meant. She took a sharp breath as she realized and looked up at Asha with a mixture of wonder and shock on her face.

Twenty-one thousand plus the seventy-nine thousand and one she got from Meeks added up to exactly one hundred thousand and one dollars. It was the magic figure she'd always thought she needed to start a new life.

Maybe he had been an angel after all.

19

Solomon managed to catch a ride in a big rig heading east just as the sun was starting to climb high enough in the sky to fry everything beneath it. The driver was a grizzled bear of a man who went by the name of Aces and had a belly so large he could practically use it to steer with. He was hauling a load of lumber to Galveston and was happy to take Solomon the whole way for the company, though he was not exactly the talkative type, which suited Solomon just fine. After the briefest of 'hello's and 'where you headed?'s they settled into a comfortable silence with only the sound of the road and a Christian Rock station for company, filling the miles with upbeat songs about being lost, being wretched, seeking love and finding Jesus. Jesus lay at the end of every journey, it seemed. Maybe that's who he'd find in France.

Solomon slipped his finger inside the flap of his jacket and felt the rough edges of the gold embroidery that spelled out in French – *This suit was made to treasure for Mr Solomon Creed* – and gave the address in the south of France of the tailor who'd made it. Solomon had no memory of ever visiting France or of having the suit made. But he figured that the tailor must have spent time with him, taken his measurements, discussed fabrics and finishes, taken details of payment. He must have known Solomon and might therefore be able to help him remember who he was. Maybe he could even help him understand why he knew what statue stood in Idaho Springs, or how he could move faster than a striking snake, or smell the oil on a shotgun held by a man hiding in the shadows of a cave. He'd smelled the man too, and known who it was before he stepped into view. That was why he'd told the lie about the name carved on the wall, another little untruth to make amends for the one he'd told earlier, a lie to cover the lie deVaca had told five hundred years earlier. Two wrongs actually making a right.

He hoped that Rita did not dwell too much on what she thought she may have lost by selling the land to Meeks, because the truth was she'd lost nothing. The land was next to worthless and Meeks had paid at least double what it was worth.

'Hungry?' Aces barked from the driver's seat.

Solomon considered the question. His steak dinner was more than half a day behind him now and the night he'd had and miles of walking after had long since burned it all off.

'Getting there,' he said.

'There's a place up ahead that does a mean burrito and a fair cup of coffee. How's that sound?'

It sounded great but there was a problem. Solomon found the worn quarter in his pocket, all the money he had in the world and not nearly enough to buy himself a meal, let alone the driver whose kindness he was currently enjoying.

'This place ahead,' he said. 'Will it be busy?'

'Should be at this time of day.'

Solomon nodded and smiled. Lots of people. That was good. It only worked if there was a sizeable crowd.

'Then I'm buying,' Solomon said.

Aces glanced over at him. 'You sure?'

Solomon nodded. 'Least I can do to say thanks for the ride.'

Aces looked unconvinced. 'You got money?'

Solomon felt the worn surface of the *bicentennial* quarter between his thumb and finger.

'Not yet,' he said. Then he looked up as a sign flashed past.

Galveston 542 miles

He'd be at the ocean by nightfall, in France within a few days. And then . . .?

The radio continued to play, songs of journeys that all ended at Jesus. But Solomon didn't want to find Him at the end of his journey. What he wanted was the answer to the simplest and also the most complex question of all.

Who am I?

Author's Note

This short story actually started life as a novel.

I'd handed in the first draft of *Solomon Creed* (called *The Searcher* in the US and Canada) and was drumming my fingers, anxiously waiting for notes and feedback and all the stuff that seems to take forever once the heavy lifting of actually finishing a novel is done. And while I waited and paced I started to think about where Solomon would go to next and how he might get there. I knew he was heading to France, because the tailor-made suit jacket he wore in book one had been made there and it had a label with an address stitched into it. The first book also ended with him walking away from the town of Redemption, Arizona, heading for a port and a ship that might take him to Europe to find the tailor who made it, hoping he in turn might be able to tell him who he was.

But there's a lot of distance between Arizona and the south of France, a lot of miles to cover, a lot of trouble to potentially get into, particularly for a man with no money, no passport and no idea who he is. And, as the main job of a thriller writer is to take their lead character, give them an objective, then make it as hard as possible for them to achieve it, this journey seemed filled with dark potential, so I started to write.

I picked up Solomon a few hundred miles east of where book one left off and figured he'd be tired and hungry so I led him into a roadside diner, set up the idea of the wager that would win him a free meal and wrote the story up to where he deciphers the petroglyphs on the photograph but can't see the whole message. At this point I didn't know what the rest of the message would say and, as it turned out, I wouldn't get to find out for another year, because this was the exact moment I got notes back on book one and had to dive back into those.

It was during the course of this second draft that it dawned on me how a road trip across Texas would be hot and dry and deserty and therefore very similar in location and feel to the Arizona of book one. So I left Solomon in the diner, waiting for the steak dinner he'd just won, and started the second book with him arriving at the small town in the south of France where his suit had been made instead.

Fast forward another year or so and I'm back to drumming my fingers waiting for first draft notes on that book (*The Boy Who Saw*) and my mind drifted back to the Solomon I had abandoned in that roadside diner, still hungry, still tired, still waiting for the steak dinner he'd won by deciphering the petro-glyphs, and it finally came to me what the rest of the message should say. So I dove back in and finished the story.

The result, *Broken Promise*, works perfectly well as a neatly self-contained story, so if you haven't read any of the *Solomon Creed* novels and don't intend to then don't worry. However it also works as a bridge between the first two books, and gives a little more insight into the mysterious Solomon.

So if you're intrigued as to what Solomon got up to in Arizona before he arrived at Bobby D's diner then you can find out everything in *Solomon Creed* (*The Searcher*). Similarly if you want to find out what happens to him after his Texas adventure, and see if he finally catches up with the French tailor then *The Boy Who Saw* will reveal all.

For any other information on new books, film and TV projects, and anything else story related then check out my website or why not sign up for my bookclub – I have been known to give stuff away.

Either way, thank you for reading this story. I'm really happy with the way it turned out, though possibly not quite as happy as Solomon is that he finally got to eat his steak dinner.

Simon Toyne

Feb 2018

If you enjoyed *Broken Promise*, read on for an exclusive extract from the next Solomon Creed thriller:

THE BOY WHO SAW

If you enjoyed this book, read on for an exclusive extract from the next Solomon Creed thriller.

THE BOY WHO SAW

1

Nothing else smells like blood.

Blood mixed with fear is something else again. Josef Engel had not smelled it in over seventy years – seventy years and he still remembered it like the years had been nothing. And this time the smell was coming from him.

He stared down at his shrunken body, his head too heavy to lift, old skin drooping like canvas over the frame of his ribs. Blood dripped vivid against the white of it, leaking from cuts in his chest that formed the Star of David. Other wounds tickled as they bled, slashes on his back where he'd been whipped, puncture wounds from something that had pinched his flesh together to cause fresh pain when he thought he'd already felt every kind there was. The pain was everything now, burning like fire through flesh that remained oddly slack and useless.

The man had come right before closing, walking into the shop and embracing Josef like an old friend. Josef had embraced him back, surprised by the action of this man dressed all in black like a shadow. Then he had felt the pinprick on his neck and tried to pull away, but the shadow man had held him tight and a cold numbness had quickly spread out from the pinprick and into his whole body. He had tried to call for help but it had come out as a drooling moan and his head fell forward on neck muscles no longer able to support the weight of his skull. There was no one around to hear anyway and the man must have known, for he had not been agitated or hurried as he calmly steered Josef to the centre of his atelier through the headless mannequins. He had slumped to the floor in the centre of the room, his arthritic knees cracking like gunshots, another memory from seventy years ago.

Josef had watched the man's shadow, cast by the skylights above, moving on the polished wooden floor as he removed Josef's shirt. A blade had appeared close to his eyes, turning slowly so the light caught the sharpness of its edge before it moved to his chest and cut through white flesh down to the bone, the blood welling around the blade and dripping down his front to the floor. He had watched it all and gasped at the explosions of pain the blade drew from him, wondering how so much agony could be contained in his old body, and why the drugs that had numbed his muscles did nothing to block the pain. He was a prisoner in his own flesh, feeling everything but incapable of doing anything to stop it. Warmth spread over him as first his blood then his bladder and bowels emptied. When the smell of that hit him he had started to cry because the humiliation was painful too.

Josef had not been this afraid since the war, when pain and death had been commonplace in the labour camps. He had escaped death then but now it had caught up with him. He watched its shadow move away across the polished wooden floor, heard the front door being unlocked and hoped that maybe the shadow man was leaving. But the door was relocked and the shadow returned and something was placed on the floor in front of him.

Tears sprang to Josef's eyes as he read the faded gold lettering on the wooden sewing machine box – *Pfaff*. It was the same make as the machine he had learned to sew on, before war had come and the world had gone dark, when all he'd wanted to do was listen to the purr of the busy needle and make beautiful things with it. Holes had been drilled in the curved top of the box and a small hatch fitted on one side with a sliding bolt keeping it shut. A faint scratching was coming from inside.

'*Du weißt warum dies dir passiert ist?*'

The man's German was accented and Josef didn't recognize the voice. He tried to look up again but his head was still too heavy.

'You know why this has happened to you?' the voice repeated, and a phone appeared in front of Josef's face, the light from the screen too bright in the evening gloom.

'*Erinnerst du dich hieran?*' the voice asked.

Josef squinted against the brightness and looked at the black-and-white photograph displayed on the phone.

'*Erinnerst du dich hieran?*' the voice repeated. 'Remember this?'

Josef did remember.

A hand swiped the screen and more photographs appeared, stark images of terrible things Josef had witnessed with his own eyes: piles of bodies in mass graves; skeletons behind wire fences, on their knees in the mud, too weak to stand, their bony shoulders tenting striped uniforms, shaved heads hanging forward while men in grey uniforms stood over them with whips and guns or the strained leashes of snarling dogs in their leather-gloved hands.

'You should have died in the camp,' the voice said. 'We should have wiped away the stain of you back then when we had the chance.'

Josef stared into eyes sunk deep in skull-like faces and imagined bony hands reaching out for him across the distance of seventy lost years, and pushing into his chest.

115

'*Der bleiche Mann,*' he whispered, his numbed tongue blurring the words.

The shadow on the floor moved closer. 'Tell me about him. Tell me about the pale man.'

'*Er kommt,*' Josef replied, his tongue wrapping around a language he had not spoken in decades. 'He is coming.' His mind was drifting now, fogged by the intense pain spreading out from his chest. 'He will save me *und die Anderen . . . Comme la dernière fois.* He will come and save us again.'

'*Die Anderen,*' the voice said. 'Tell me about the others. Tell me what happened back in the camp. State your name and give me your confession.'

Josef hesitated for a moment before starting to speak, the words flowing out of him in a steady stream, loosened by the drug and the feeling that as long as he continued to talk he would be allowed to live. 'I kept it safe,' Josef said when he had finished his confession, his hands tingling as the drug began to wear off. He reached up to where the skeleton fingers continued to tear at his heart and pain bloomed.

'What did you keep safe?'

'The list,' Josef gasped.

'Tell me about the list.'

'*Der weiße Anzug,*' Josef clutched his chest and pushed back against the pain. 'The white suit. We promised to keep it safe and we did. All these years we kept it safe.'

Josef managed to raise his head a little and stared up at the outline of his killer silhouetted against the skylights. The man reached down and Josef closed his eyes and braced himself for some new pain, but something touched his face and he opened his eyes again and saw a white tissue in the man's hand, dabbing at the blood around his eyes as gently as a mother cleaning jam from a child's mouth. Josef started to weep at this unexpected

116

gesture of kindness. He could smell disinfectant on the man's hand and saw that he was wearing thin surgical gloves the same colour as skin.

'Remember the camp,' the man asked, 'remember what it was like at the very end, all those bodies piling up and no one left to bury them?' He moved over to the wooden box and twisted the tissue until blood squeezed out between his latex-covered fingers. 'Do you remember the rats?' He bent down and fed the tapered end of the tissue into one of the larger holes and the scratching intensified. 'All those walking skeletons but the rats never went hungry, did they?' The tissue twitched and was tugged inside the box with a flurry of squeaks and scratching. 'I caught these rats near a chicken farm almost a week ago. They haven't eaten much since – only each other. I wonder how many there are left?' He reached down for the bolt holding the hatch shut and Josef felt panicked pain explode in his chest. 'Or you could tell me more about the white suit and I'll keep the box shut.'

Tears dripped down Josef's face, stinging as they salted the wounds on his chest. The pain was unbearable now. He had never escaped the camp, not really. He had carried it with him all this time, and now it was bursting out of him again.

'Tell me about the suit.' The man slid the latch across but held the door shut.

'The pale man,' Josef said, shaking uncontrollably, his breathing shallow. 'We made it for him.' He dragged his eyes from the box and looked desperately over at the door as if hoping he might be standing there. 'He said he would come for it. He said it would keep us safe. We made a deal. He will—'

Pain erupted inside Josef, a jagged explosion of glass and fire that forced all the air from his lungs. His eyes flew wide and he crumpled to the floor, gasping for breath but getting none. He lay on his side and saw a thimble lying deep under one of the workbenches, worn and familiar and bent to the shape of his finger over long years of work, the same thimble he'd had back in the camp, back in that cellar. He had lost it a month or so ago and looked for it everywhere. And there it was. And here was he. The pain was consuming him now. Swallowing him whole. Pulling him down. His killer dropped to the floor, cutting off his view of the lost thimble, and Josef felt a pressure on his neck and smelled rubber and disinfectant as fingers checked for a pulse. Josef's view shifted as he was rolled on to his back and he heard a thud and felt a fist hammer down on the centre of his chest, heard a rib crack but didn't feel anything because the pain inside him was already too great.

Josef looked beyond the silhouette of the man and up to the sky where thin white clouds slid across the deepening blue sky. He had worked in this room for over forty years but this was the first time he could remember looking up. He had never looked at the sky in the camp either, had always found it too painful to gaze up at such simple, boundless beauty when all around him was ugliness and horror.

The man continued to pound on his chest but Josef knew it was pointless. There was no saving him now. The man in the white suit was not coming. He would not cheat Death a second time. He took a last, deep, jagged breath. Stared up at the indigo sky. And closed his eyes.

* * *

He stopped pounding on the brittle chest and looked down at the tailor's broken body. He could see the outline of ribs beneath the dark blood and papery skin and watched for a while to see if they moved. They didn't.

He took another tissue from his pocket, balled it up and wiped it around the slashed, wet edges of the star then stood and moved through the silent, headless crowd of mannequins to a blank section of wall on the far side of the atelier. He pressed the bloody tissue to the wall, dabbing it on the chalky surface and returning to the body whenever the tissue ran dry. It was full dark by the time he had finished but he could see what he'd written on the wall. Death was not enough for *Die Anderen,* they also had to know it was coming and feel its shadow on their backs, exactly as it had been in the camps.

He began to search the atelier. No one was due back here until morning, so he took his time, working steadily and searching the main house too, looking for the list and the suit Josef Engel had mentioned. He found nothing.

When he had finished, he stood in the centre of the atelier and looked down at the still figure on the floor, listening to the scratching and squeaking rats and the clock striking midnight in the hallway. He wondered if Josef had wound the clock that morning, not realizing it would keep ticking after his heart had stopped. Time had run out for the old man, like it did for everyone in the end – like it would for him soon enough.

He felt tired and empty and the pain in his head was starting to grow but he wasn't finished here, not quite. He moved over to the wooden box, lifted the hatch on the side and dark shapes poured out, scraps of darkness scrabbling across the polished floorboards towards the scent of blood. They swarmed over the body, fighting and squeaking as they tugged at the cooling flesh and each other as they went into a feeding frenzy.

The man watched them for a long time. Listening to the tick of the clock and thinking about the list and what he had missed, and everything he had to do before all of this would be over.

2

Madjid Lellouche snicked away another withered vine before looking up. He knew he would be in trouble if he was seen to stop work, even for a moment, yet something made him pause and turn – and then he saw him.

The man was maybe fifty feet away, passing in and out of view between the plane trees lining the Roman road built at the same time as the vineyards. The road was directly behind where Madjid was working and lower down the hill, so no movement could have caught his eye. He was also far enough away that the sound of footsteps could not have reached him, even if the wind had been in the right direction, which it wasn't. There was no wind today anyway, only sunlight and the melting ground mist and the promise of another day of solid heat that would sit like a boulder on his back as he worked, drying the ground to dust between the green lines of vines.

Madjid shielded his eyes against the glare of the morning sun and watched the man pass in and out of view between the trees, moving through the mist that pooled in the lower valley. He was pale and slender and tall and wore a light suit jacket that looked formal and old, and his hair was white though he seemed young, moving with the smooth grace of a dancer and not the stiffness of a man of advanced years. Madjid listened out through the whine of insects for the sound of his footsteps and heard instead the snap of a twig behind him, and the swish of a cane cutting through the air followed by the sharp burn of sudden pain.

'The fuck I'm paying you for?'

Madjid turned and raised his arms against the next blow. '*Désolé*,' he called out, backing away from the man with the stick in his hand. '*Désolé, monsieur.*' Madjid bumped against the vines and a handful of grapes pattered on to the dust, their skins wrinkled and spotted with blight.

'Sorry doesn't get the work done.' The cane sliced back down and Madjid felt the bite of it on his forearm and fell to his knees. He stared up at the large, sweaty figure of Michel LePoux through a gap in his raised arms and saw anger burning in piggy eyes staring out from a bright red face. '*Désolé*, Monsieur LePoux,' he said.

The cane rose again and Madjid closed his eyes against the blow. Heard the swish of it coming back down and the slap of it striking skin, only this time he felt no pain. He opened his eyes and looked up. LePoux was standing right in front of him, silhouetted against the bleached blue sky – and so was the man from the road.

'Ouch,' he said, in a voice that was low like thunder and soft as the wind through the vines. '*Ça fait mal*' – *That hurt*. He stretched the word '*mal*', like the locals did, and it came out sounding more like '*mel*'.

LePoux tugged at his cane, trying to free it from the man's grip but he held on to it with little apparent effort, despite the fact that LePoux was twice the weight of the stranger. LePoux stopped tugging and glared at the man. 'You're trespassing.'

121

'And you are violently assaulting someone,' the stranger replied, 'which of those crimes is the greater, do you suppose?'

'Crime?' LePoux spat on the ground. 'There is no crime. This man is mine and what I do with *my* property on *my* land is *my* business.'

He yanked the stick again and the stranger let go, sending LePoux stumbling backwards. He grabbed at the vines and more shrivelled grapes pattered to the ground. The stranger dipped down to pick one up. 'Your country banned slavery in 1831.' He crushed the grape, sniffed the pink juice, then licked the end of his finger and looked up at LePoux. 'So how can this man be your property?'

LePoux stood up and pulled his sweat-damp shirt away from his skin. 'I don't know who you are, monsieur. Your accent's local but I know that you're not. I know everyone around here – law, lawyers, judges, everyone – but I don't know you and you're trespassing on my land, so if I want to chase you off it with a stick or a shotgun, no one here would say a thing against it.'

He raised his cane again but the stranger didn't move. 'How long has this land been yours?' he asked.

'My family's been here for five generations,' LePoux replied, puffing out his chest.

The stranger stared at LePoux and shook his head slowly. 'Pity you won't make it to a sixth.'

LePoux's face flushed red and his knuckles whitened. He lashed out with the cane, bringing it down hard on the stranger. LePoux was fast but the stranger was faster. He stepped aside as quick as blinking and the cane smacked on to the ground where he had been standing. LePoux stumbled forward, unbalanced by the force of the blow, and the stranger stamped down on the middle of his stick, breaking it in two with a sound like snapping bone, then twisted and kicked LePoux so hard he flew right through the vines and landed in the next row in a tangle of wire and foliage.

122

He smoothed his suit jacket down and held out his hand to Madjid and he felt the strength in it as he pulled him to his feet. His hand was solid like marble and strong like a blacksmith's, though with none of the coarseness of work upon it, and he seemed both old and young, his white hair ageing him but his smooth skin making him seem youthful. He could have been any age between twenty and sixty, though his eyes were old and black and deep, like staring into a well.

'The next town,' the man asked in his low voice, 'what's it called?'

'Cordes,' Madjid replied. 'Cordes-sur-Ciel.'

He nodded. 'And is there a tailor there?'

'Monsieur Engel.'

'What about a man or a place called *Magellan*?'

Madjid frowned and searched his memory. He wanted to help this man who'd helped him but the name meant nothing. 'I'm sorry,' he said. 'I've never heard that name.' He felt bad, like he had let him down in some way.

The stranger nodded and frowned. 'Thank you for your time,' he said, then he turned back to LePoux. 'Your land is rotten,' he said, plucking a leaf from a branch and holding it up so the sun lit up the orange and black tiger stripes on the green leaf. 'You have esca in all your vines but, given the sorry state of your land and the way you treat your workers, I would imagine you have neither the funds nor the reputation to get the help you need to cut it out. Your harvest will fail and you will be forced to sell, sooner rather than later.' He dropped the leaf and turned back to Madjid. 'You should leave,' he said. 'There's nothing for you here but pain.' Then he tipped his head in a courtly way and walked away.

Madjid watched him leave, moving through the vines and back towards the road. Behind him he heard crashing and huffing as LePoux scrambled back to his feet.

'Get back to work,' he said, picking up the broken halves of his cane and looking at them before throwing them to the ground.

Madjid looked around at the vines, the tiger-striped leaves glowing orange on almost every plant. The stranger was right, the crop was already lost. And when rot had claimed the whole harvest, LePoux would blame him, call him lazy and beat him as he drove him from the land without pay. He needed to get away from here. It was so obvious he felt like he had woken from a spell. He had been blinded by his lack of options and by his blind faith in hard work. He looked back at the stranger who had opened his eyes. He was almost at the road now. 'What's your name, monsieur?' he called after him.

'Solomon,' the man replied without looking round, his voice as soft as before but carrying back to Madjid as clearly as if he had shouted it. 'My name is Solomon Creed.'

3

Commandant Benoît Amand of the Police Nationale felt the buzz of an incoming call in his pocket. He ignored it, reaching out instead to wipe a finger across the swastika someone had sprayed on the Jewish memorial, the thick black paint dripping on to the names carved into granite remembering those who'd been rounded up and transported to the death camps on the night of 26 August 1942. He heard the crunch of footsteps across the boules court and the slop of water in a bucket.

'You want to take pictures first?' a voice asked.

'No,' Amand said, moving past him and heading across La Place 26th Aout towards Café Belloq on the far side of the square. 'I want you to scrub away all trace of it.'

The breakfast crowd were sitting in the shade of a wide, red awning, drinking their coffee and staring at their phones and newspapers. A few were looking over at him. Jean-Luc Belloq was one of them. He had been polishing the same glass with his apron ever since Amand had arrived.

Amand reached into his pocket, his hand pushing past his now silent phone to the bottle of glycerine pills, and unscrewed the lid one-handed so Belloq wouldn't see. He passed the half-constructed stage, part of the planned celebrations to mark seventy years since the end of the Second World War. The banners weren't up yet, otherwise the vandal might have defaced them too. The rest of the square was deserted, the chess tables and boules courts not yet populated by the old men who used the square as an al fresco social club. He palmed a glycerine caplet, popped it into his mouth under cover of a cough, manoeuvred it under his tongue and immediately felt the tightness in his chest melt away. His phone buzzed again, rattling against the pill bottle, but he let it ring, focusing instead on his breathing like his doctor had taught him as he mounted the stone steps to the café and nodded a greeting to the few diners who weren't tourists.

'Commandant,' Jean-Luc said, polishing the glass like it would never be clean. 'I still can't get used to the way you look. Let me get you a coffee.' He made to turn then stopped and struck his forehead theatrically with his palm. 'Sorry. No stimulants, right? Must be so frustrating to lose all that weight and still have the heart of a sumo.'

The phone in Amand's pocket stopped buzzing and the pill under his tongue continued to dilate his veins. 'What time did you open this morning?' he asked.

'Around six, same as always.'

'Notice anything suspicious?'

'Suspicious how?'

'Like someone over by the memorial plaque spraying a swastika on it?' Jean-Luc shook his head. 'Anyone else around?' He continued to shake his head. 'What about the café, anyone in before you?'

'I'm always first in.'

'When did you notice the graffiti?'

'I didn't.' Jean-Luc nodded at a waitress cleaning a couple of tables at the rear of the terrace. 'She did. She told me. I called you.'

'Does *she* have a name?'

'Probably. We have a high turnover of staff here and I'm not good with names.'

Amand nodded. Café Belloq was notorious for working its staff into the ground and paying them peanuts. 'Mind if I talk to her?' He started to head over and Jean-Luc followed. Amand stopped and turned to him. 'Alone, if you don't mind.'

Belloq looked like he did mind but the phone started ringing inside the café, the trilling bells like an echo from the past. It was an old Bakelite model, so ancient it had become fashionable again, a result of meanness rather than forward thinking or style.

'Shouldn't you get that?' Amand said. Jean-Luc glanced at the waitress, then turned and marched away. Amand waited until he disappeared inside the café before walking over to the waitress.

'Mademoiselle?' he said, stopping at her table. 'I'm Benoît Amand from the Police Nationale.' She looked up in alarm from the croissant crumbs she was sweeping on to a plate. 'Don't worry, you're not in any trouble. What's your name?'

Her eyes flicked over to the café where Jean-Luc was visible through a window, talking on the phone and looking in their direction. 'Mariella,' she murmured.

'Mariella, Monsieur Belloq says it was you who spotted the graffiti on the plaque.' She gave a tiny nod. 'What time was this?'

'When I was setting the tables out. Six thirty maybe.'

'And when did you tell Monsieur Belloq about it?'

'I told him as soon as I spotted it.'

'And was anyone else around at that time?'

'No.'

'Thank you, Mariella.'

She nodded and scurried away, grateful for the release.

Amand headed into the café, glancing over at the man with the bucket scrubbing away at the memorial plaque, the swastika now concealed beneath thick suds that dripped grey down the stonework.

'He's here,' Belloq said, holding the phone out to him the moment he stepped into the bar.

'Is that clock right?' Amand asked, nodding at the grandmother clock that had kept time in Café Belloq since before the war.

Belloq nodded. 'I reset it each morning when I wind it. Why?'

'Because I'm interested to know why it took you three hours to call us after you first saw a Nazi symbol painted on a Jewish memorial outside your café.'

Belloq shrugged. 'Didn't think it was important.'

Amand took the phone and caught the smell of tobacco soaked into the black plastic over decades. 'Amand.'

'Why aren't you answering your phone?'

Amand stiffened, picking up on the tension in the sergeant's voice. 'What's up, Henri?'

'It's Josef Engel. His cleaner just called. She's hysterical, said that there are rats everywhere. Parra is already on his way to Engel's atelier. She said that he's been murdered.'

4

Solomon's hand stung where he'd caught the cane, a burning sensation that was not entirely unpleasant. He flexed his fingers to feed the ache and let it sharpen his senses as he walked down the road. He could smell hints of the town ahead of him now, like something small and hard buried beneath the softer, blanketing smells of the countryside: stone and concrete; hot tile and cooking oil; sour sweat and hair grease and the underlying sewagey stink of almost a thousand years of human occupation.

His feet were road weary inside the scuffed rancher's boots he'd borrowed from a dead man in Arizona. They had carried him along the interstates and back roads of New Mexico and Texas, clanged on the sheet-metal deck of a container ship out of Galveston, and now trod the same straight road sandalled centurions had built two thousand years earlier. Squares of grey overlapped on the road's surface where intense summer heat and dry frozen winters had split and cracked it again and again until it had become a thing of fragments – like Solomon himself.

The town of Cordes came into view gradually, emerging from the mist like a mountain castle at the end of the patchwork road.

Castellated walls circled the summit, the thick stone worn with age and blending into the jagged outcrops of limestone from the original Puech de Mordagne. Stone buildings clung to the side of it like barnacles on a shark's fin and Solomon could read the history of the town's development in its architecture, oldest buildings at the top, youngest at the base, with narrow winding streets and long flights of stone steps linking the different levels. A thin tower rose up at the top, the name of the church it belonged to whispering in his head, prompted by the sight of it: L'Eglise Saint-Michel – the Church of St Michael.

Solomon had seen the town before, in a dream. He slept little and dreamed hardly at all and when he did it was usually the same dream, the one of the mirror that showed no reflection. But once, in his cramped bunk in the galley of the transport ship, he had slipped into slumber and seen this place, misty and indistinct, exactly as it appeared now.

Cordes-sur-Ciel – Cordes on Sky – named for the phenomenon Solomon was now witnessing where the town seemed to float on the valley mist.

The town continued to materialize from the mist as he drew closer, and more facts surfaced in his mind:

Founded 1222 by the Comte de Toulouse . . . Almost ended by plague in 1348 . . . Battered by the Hundred Years War in the fourteenth century and the Wars of Religion in the sixteenth.

Market town. Merchant centre. Textiles and wool, then indigo and Broderie Anglais lace. The small crocodiles on a famous French designer brand had been made here.

Tourist town now, teeming in the long summer months with people drawn by its history and weather and the beautiful stone houses with views over vine-covered valleys.

The information cascaded through Solomon's head, every fact correct but nothing that told him how he might be connected to the place. That part of his memory was gone, along with every other detail of who he was or might once have been. Whenever he focused his know-it-all mind on thoughts of himself, it fell silent – no facts, no memories. It was like staring into the mirror in his dream, the one that reflected nothing. All he had were fragments and questions.

He unbuttoned his tailored suit jacket and looked at the label stitched inside:

Ce costume a été fait au trésor pour M. Solomon Creed – This suit was made to treasure for Mr Solomon Creed.

The gold thread shone in the morning sunlight, spelling out the address where the suit had been made around the edge of the label:

13, Rue Obscure, Cordes-sur-Ciel, Tarn.

He let the flap of the jacket fall back down, the cut fitting the slender contours of his body perfectly. This was the place where someone had measured him and adjusted the cut until it fit him like a second skin. Here someone must have taken payment, perhaps made arrangements for its delivery, noting down an address and a name, tiny fragments of his lost history that might lead all the way back to who he really was, like stones through a dark forest. He was incomplete and so was the story of the clothes he wore.

Ce costume, the label said – this suit – yet he only had the jacket.

He re-buttoned it, the scents of his long journey trapped in the fabric – the salt of the ocean, diesel fumes and rice-wine vinegar, horseradish and tobacco smoke. He flexed his hand and carried on walking towards the town and the tailor he had travelled over five-thousand miles to find. Towards the address stitched in gold on a label. Towards answers.

The scent of the town was stronger now he could see it, the

smell of the people who lived here soaked into the stone over countless centuries and carrying on the misty breeze like pollen. Solomon breathed deeply, identifying each scent as easily as a florist enumerating the fragrance of different flowers. He knew the cause of each too, the emotion beneath each enzyme: fear, regret, happiness, longing . . . and a new scent, an unusual odour, sharp and metallic, that seemed more familiar to him than all the other smells blowing his way on the shifting breeze. It was a smell that made his heart thrum faster and the brand on his shoulder ache in a way that told him it was significant – the smell of freshly spilled human blood.